SWEIN: THE DANISH KING

An Earls of Mercia Side Story

By MJ Porter

Cover design by MJ Porter
Cover image by Illustration 21760792 © Algol - Dreamstime.com

CONTENTS

PROLOGUE

The babe screamed as it was pressed into his father's arms. The man looked around the small, warm room uncomfortably. He'd never been a man to pick up other men's children, to talk to them and play games. He was a grim man, faced with the task of keeping his fledgeling kingdom together. He accepted that he needed children, but what should he do now that he held his firstborn son in his arms?

He was nothing more than a reminder that life was bloody and short and that he would have to nurture the small being until it was old enough to replace him.

It wasn't a pleasant thought for a young man more interested in war and his kingdom than anything else.

He'd hoped he'd feel a spark of emotion for the tiny bundle in his arms, but its screeching was giving him a headache, and with the boy's scrunched up face, still blood streaked, he couldn't determine what sort of man the babe would grow to be. He needed to see the child's eyes, to peer into its depth, but it wouldn't open them, and he felt his frustration mount as he held his son.

Awkwardly, he patted the babe's bottom, as he'd seen others do, and rocked it gently in his massive arms. He was a warrior, not a nursemaid.

The child still cried, while his wife looked at him in concern, her face bleached of all colour by the exertion she'd just put into bringing the tiny life into the world. He wanted to go to her, thank her, ensure she was well, but instead, the babe had been placed into his arms, and he knew he needed to do something to make his wife think he could at least love the child.

She was more than aware of his feelings towards the tiny bundle. She'd teased him when he'd grumbled that she was to be responsible for his replacement, but her good-natured tolerance had strained, as her belly had grown fatter and fatter. She'd come to realise that he truly was angry about the whole thing. She'd thrown her hands up in the air in despair and asked him what he'd thought would happen when he'd taken her to his bed.

He'd had no answer to that.

He liked women. He wanted to bed them. He didn't like to think of the consequences. His first child, his daughter, had been but a girl and he'd managed to reconcile his thoughts towards her with little difficulty. This boy would be another matter entirely. She was not a miniature version of him but his wife. She would sway the heads of men when she was older. Not like his son.

And now he held his consequence in his arms once more, and he pulled the fur down to truly gaze at his son's face. He would call him Swein, he knew that already, but as he took in the perfectly formed features on the squalling face, he felt a jolt of worry. The child was marked. He placed his huge thumb on the brown blemish that seemed to mar his chin, wondering if it would wipe away, and when it did not, his fear grew a little.

Was this some message from his Gods? Was this punishment for not wanting the child and desiring it? For praying for another girl child? For refusing to accept his mortality?

Quickly, he stripped the crying child of its fur covering and placed him on the edge of his wife's bed. His wife watched him carefully from her expanse of furs as he explored every part of the small babe's body with his rough warrior hands, looking for other marks.

There were none.

His wife looked at him with a question in his eyes as he pointed to Swein's chin.

She raised her eyebrow at him and then grinned at the area of his concern.

"It's nothing, a birthmark. Don't worry about it."

The others in the room were becoming aware of the muted conversation between the parents. The birthing woman came to stare at the child, her expression clear as she too ran her eyes over the baby, and then picked up the small crying specimen and looked him all over from head to toe, much as his father had done.

Content that there were no other issues, she handed the child back to his mother and watched with a wry smile on her face as the babe sought and found his mother's nipple and began to suck contentedly.

The father watched on impassively.

No one else seemed concerned.

"He'll just have to grow a nice beard," the birthing woman said into the sudden silence. "Other than that, he's hale and hearty. A good, healthy boy. He'll be an asset to you," she added as an afterthought. She too knew what Harald thought of the child he'd just been presented with. There had been much discussion amongst the women about how to offer the child to the father in the best possible light to stop his fears and worries. The birthmark was a tiny blemish on a perfectly well-made babe. The mother had done well.

"A beard?" Harald said in surprise. "It'll be years before he has a beard and until then, all men will see his mark."

The birthing woman bent over his wife at his angry tone and once more glanced at the child.

"It looks to me as though it's a perfect little hammer. It looks as though the Gods have marked him. Indeed, he's a fortunate child."

Harald rushed forward to once more gaze at the suckling child. He turned his head from one side to the other and then he stared at his wife, swallowing against the fear he felt when he looked at his son.

"I think you're right. He's been marked by the Gods for great things in this life."

His wife relaxed as he spoke and he finally appreciated how much she'd feared what he might say next. After all, he was the father. He could have demanded the child be exposed, and in the howling wind and snow that swirled outside in the bitter chill winter, it would not have taken the child long to die if it had been exposed to the elements.

He bent down and placed a kiss on first his wife's forehead and then on his son's smaller face.

The child smelled of newness and death all intermingled.

Once more, he swallowed his fear and plastered a smile on his face so that his wife would not see his worry and irrational fear.

This child would bring him great problems and trouble.

He knew it.

He reached around his neck and pressed the small hammer that lay against his chest.

What trick were the Gods playing on him now?

CHAPTER 1

Fyrkat, Denmark
AD970

He watched his father angrily. His father was a huge man, a warrior, his hair growing grey and his beard flecked with white. His blue eyes were sharp and noticed everything. His clothing was rich and yet he wore a continually downcast expression, as though life was a continual disappointment to him.

Once more Swein had been berated for the smallest of transgressions. Any other father would have been proud of a son for defending the weak and innocent, but not his father. No, he cared more about the dishonour done to the man responsible for whipping the small child, than the injured child, and now he was ensuring that his son was being made to pay for his honourable actions.

His young stepmother was watching him with downcast eyes. He knew she was as dismayed as he was. He also knew that he couldn't rely on her to step into the fray for him. She wasn't scared of his father but neither was she prepared to intervene for the children of his first wife. Until she produced her own children, her position at the king's court was uncomfortable. That he already had nearly grown sons by his first wife only added to her difficulties. He could almost have pitied her if she hadn't been so unprepared to help him.

His father was a strict man. Other men admired him and his inability to compromise. Swein found it frustrating and more often than not, disagreed with everything that his father tried to do. He might only be a youth, only just learning his way around weapons and statecraft but he'd been watching men all his life, and he knew how to tempt the best from them. It seemed as though his father had never learned the lesson, and probably never would.

He might only be young, with no more than ten summers to his name, but he saw, and he knew far more than he probably should. He was aware that his father was not a great leader of men because of his abilities, but more because he scared them into doing what he wanted, and if that failed, he relied on one of his more congenial oath sworn men to smooth over any difficulties.

Finulf was a good-natured giant, so used to putting men at ease that Swein didn't think he even noticed he was doing it anymore. He liked Finulf, the most of all the men within his father's hall. For those who were less jolly, the angular Harth could convince them to do the king's actions. Swein wondered if there was any part of the hard man that was soft and pliable. He spoke sharply. His face was square and his body, when he moved it, was lightning fast.

His father was usually able to manipulate events that happened around him. He was not a great innovator, but that didn't mean he couldn't take advantage of circumstances that were favourable to him when Finulf's good nature and Harth's sharp voice failed to make men bend as he bid them.

His father was king by dint of his birth, not because of his abilities.

Yes, he might have claimed more land for his family within and without Denmark, and he might have made his neighbours fear the might of the Danish men, but for Swein he would always simply be a harsh man who governed with his fists and his sword, not with his heart and his mind. Even his supposed conversion to the new Christian religion had been accomplished through violence and pain, dragging his young son with him to ensure that his marked chin would be forgiven by the new God, the Christian God, the God his father had been convinced would give him what he wanted. Swein only wished he knew what that was.

Nothing his father ever did was done with the thoughts of others in mind. He didn't care who died to enable him to get what he wanted. He had a goal in mind, and he strove with his every breath, his every movement to achieve the aim. It was abundantly clear to Swein that he was not a part of his father's achievements. He was simply a cross to be born, a sin to deal with.

That his father was so successful only made the injustice of it harder to tolerate for Swein. It went against the Christian teachings his father made him learn, and it went against the poems and saga tales that the skalds muttered from their place within the king's hall. Nothing was as it should be and the injustice of it all burned deep inside his slight, youthful frame. He wished himself as renowned as Finulf so that he could attack his father and show him who was right and who was wrong. But his body refused to grow as he wanted it to, and he knew he'd have to wait long years to punish his father for his slights and his taunts, and more than anything, his total ignorance of his children.

Neither was Swein alone in his hatred of his father. His brother and sisters shared it. Thrya was his older sister, more a woman now and soon to be married, his younger brother Haakon and his sister, Gytha, the sweet baby of the family. She'd been his mother's pride and joy until her untimely death barely a year ago. His father had wasted no time in finding himself a new wife.

Thrya thought little of the woman, but then, really there was so little difference in age between the two that Swein could understand her unease. She must hope that their father didn't marry her to a man old enough to be her father, as cruel as her father could be.

But his mind wondered, and he was busy trying to decide how he could punish his father for the outrage he felt. He watched him with narrowed eyes and refused to do anything to stop the blood that dripped from his bloody nose, onto his lips and the floor beneath him. He stood proudly. His father was a mean man, one that his followers were uneasy around in moments such as these when he showed his true self and dropped all pretense of being a caring father.

Swein thought he'd never learnt to love his children. He watched them with equal parts fear and jealousy but no love. It confused him. He'd loved his own father. That was clear to see. If he hadn't why would he have gone to all the trouble of having him disinterred from his grave mound and reburied within his wooden church that he'd had built when he'd accepted his new religion?

Swein wondered why he'd never learnt to love his children. It bothered him more than it should, and he knew it was against his father's new Christian teaching. For now, he was only relieved that his father demanded his attention within the new wooden church at Hedeby but prayed no further into his thoughts. He'd long since lost the fight as to which religion he should follow. His father said all men should have a choice, but not in his family. No, his wife and his children, they all had to pray to their Christian God.

The hall they were within was at the centre of the fortress his father had built at Fyrkat. Swein thought the fortress was a thing of beauty. Within the fort, men could live with their families and train to protect their king all at the same time. There was no need to call men from their families and have them worried about them. Clearly, Harald understood the motivations of his men without sharing their familial bonds.

Swein liked nothing more than to escape his father's watchful eye and make his way to the four identical quarters of the fortresses. He could overhear men discussing their thoughts on their king, and women discussing men. He probably shouldn't hear half of what he did, but that never stopped him from listening carefully and filing away the information for later.

That was one of his skills. He didn't act irrationally, never. The actions that he took were always considered from as many angles as possible. Often he didn't do anything with what he learnt but keep the knowledge greedily to himself. One day he would undo his father with everything he knew or suspected about him.

One day, his father would rue his brutal treatment of him.

He sniffed, forgetting for a moment that his nose was throbbing and the pain made him wince. His young sister, sitting near to where he was standing as punishment, stuck her tongue out at him, and he gave her half a smile. She was a small thing, not at all built to withstand their father's harshness. He tried his best to shield her from their father, and he was trying to get his father's new wife to intervene for her as well.

She wasn't a healthy child, born when his mother had already been weakened by illness, although she'd survived for four long years after her birth. But she was beautiful and engaging, and he knew that he wasn't the only person within his father's household who tried to keep her safe. Even his fierce older sister would deign to watch out for her little sister, and she was almost as self-centered as their father.

He rubbed his hand across his chin, hoping to feel the faint stirring of the beard he craved to cover the mark that marred his chin and that made his father detest him even more. That his first male child was somehow marked for greatness by the Gods at his birth had fuelled his father's fears of him, and nothing anyone had said then, or since, had managed to assuage the fears of the father. All things considered, it was far easier to stay away from his father.

One day he would avenge himself on his father, make good all the slights and taunts of his childhood.

But first, he needed to be a man.

He often prayed to the God who'd marked him with his hammer on his chin, asking him to bring him strength and asking him to aid him in his endeavours. As of yet, he wasn't convinced that Thor listened to him, but that wasn't going to make him stop. He was convinced that the Old Gods were far better allies than the new Christianity. Although, and here he worried a little, he could understand why his father had made the transition. There was a strange power in which faith he followed. It brought men and women to his side who might in the past have stayed distant from him.

That worried Swein because he didn't want to become a mirror image of his father but he did want the support of as many men and women as possible. He felt sure that he would do almost anything to ensure the loyalty of his followers, if only he could gain them first.

For now, he hated his father and let his hatred build within him. He could admit to himself that there were some elements to his father's character that he admired. But that didn't mean he coveted them, and he wasn't at all convinced that he'd always respect his father, his king, a brutal man who only knew how to make men do his wishes through fear.

Swein knew there was another way, and he intended to utilise it when he became king in his own right.

CHAPTER 2
Denmark, Hedeby
AD986

S wein eyed his father angrily. He wondered if a day had ever passed that he'd not hated the old bastard. He doubted it.

His father was an old man now, well into his fifth decade but while his movements might have slowed, his mind was as active as it always had been and at the moment it was directed at Swein, and he relished the scrutiny. He imagined it was the first time his father had looked at him in nearly ten years.

Not since his difficulties with the men of the German lands beginning twelve years ago had Harald so much as acknowledged he had a son, let alone that he had two. His father had married his elder sister to Styrbjorn, the man whose sister he had himself married and Swein knew that as fearful as she'd been, she'd married well and had a far happier life than he or his father's second wife had ever had. He didn't envy her, though. She was a woman of good birth and needed a good husband. She'd had no choice in it.

What he needed was to make a name for himself, and that was what ailed his father now.

Harald was a man of action, keen to recapture his lost barrier, the Danevirke, from the grasping hands of the men on his borders. He'd not cared who he'd overstepped along the way, or hurt. It was his damn fault if in the intervening years, the years when he'd built his identical fortresses at Aggersborg, Nonnebakken and on the island of Zeeland and personally overseen their construction, that his sons had grown and made names for themselves as great warriors.

No, it was his fault that he was now presented with two strong sons, stronger than he was, and with more power at their fingertips than he'd ever had.

His father knew how to count and mint coins, how to ensure enough trees would be felled to build the ramparts and the wooden strakes around the fortresses, not to mention the building inside. His father knew how to entice men to live within those fortresses.

He seemed to have forgotten that more was needed to be a king. Swein had not. He'd watched his father every day since he was a boy, and whenever he wasn't off fighting in battles or building churches, or raising stones to the memory of his father and his mother. He knew how to rule now. He'd watched all his father's mistakes, and he was damned if he was going to let his father rule anymore.

He was too old and too destructive. Swein had decided it was time he was king. His father needed removing.

A younger man was needed to take control of the kingdom, or it threatened to disintegrate before everyone's eyes.

There were more men than Harald who wanted to be king of Denmark, his eldest son amongst them, but his son at least would honour the memory of his father, if he'd just leave, now, without any more fuss.

He watched his father with interest. He didn't seem to know what to say or what to do, not when faced with his sons and their weapons, battle ready.

The old man's eyes narrowed as he clutched the wooden sides of his ceremonial chair, and Swein steeled himself for whatever angry words would come from his mouth. His father was always keen to belittle him, even when he didn't look at him.

"I see you finally grew a beard," he eventually muttered, and Swein began to laugh, a deep sound that came from the centre of his belly and his well of inborn confidence. Was that the best he could do?

"Father, I grew my beard many, many years ago. About the time your own stopped growing."

His father sported a fine beard, but his hair had long since fallen away, and now he often looked as though he had his head on upside down. Swein didn't think the look worked well with his mean eyes and bloated nose from being broken one too many times. His father might once have been attractive. He no longer saw it, and neither did his stepmother.

Swein watched as his father's mouth opened and closed, unsure what to say.

He knew his most loyal counsellors had warned him that his sons were amassing against him and that they had thousands of supporters. His father had been too arrogant to take heed of the words, and now he was about to pay the final price for his cockiness.

"You can leave father, now, or I will chase you from this place. I'll not kill you. I'm not the sort of man to kill a defenceless old man."

He watched with satisfaction as his father flinched at hearing those words. Swein understood now that his second wife had been taken as a way to soften his worries about growing old. All he'd accomplished was to appear even older than he was when he stood or sat beside her. That she was also barren had only added to the total failure of the marriage.

His father had intended more sons, better sons than the two he already had. Swein knew it would never happen. He imagined that in taking a new wife when the old was not even cold in her grave, his father had angered his discarded Old Gods, and probably the new as well.

His second marriage had been an infertile failure, his young wife keen to bed anyone who'd have her. She was a warm and pliant woman, and Swein had often spent the night with her. Something else his father didn't know but during those nights she'd whisper of his father's harshness, of his selfish ways and his love for his stepmother made it difficult for him to allow his father to leave unharmed. He would far rather kill him, but that was not his intention.

"This is my kingdom. You have no right to demand I leave it and hand it over to you."

Swein walked towards his father. His hand placed on his short dagger at his belt. He meant it to appear menacing, but he also knew he'd never use it against his father. He might hate the man, but he'd given him life, and he would at least be grateful for that, and show some respect.

"Father," he began, his words slow and measured, he'd thought about this speech for many long years, turning the phrase over in his mind during the dark nights when his bruises had ached, or he'd struggled to breathe through his damaged ribs. "You're no longer king here. I have all the warriors from your forts, and they're here, outside now, to support me. They demand as I demand and my brother, that you leave this place. It's no longer yours. You've lost the support and the love of your people and in your place, they've chosen me to succeed you."

The sharp eyes of his father watched him, but other than that he didn't react at all to the words his son spoke to him. Swein tempered his growing anger. It would only add to Harald's pleasure in denying his son's demands if he knew how much it upset him.

He'd known it would be difficult to remove him from Hedeby but he'd also known that his play for power needed to be made here. It was symbolic. It was the home of his family. Outside the wooden church, his grandfather's body had rotted away to nothing and under the high mound his grandmother's body had also been left to decompose. His mother lay in the churchyard as well. This was the home of the House of Gorm. To become king, he needed to usurp his father's position as king in this place.

At his side his brother shuffled on his feet, catching the attention of his father. Swein suppressed a groan. His brother Haakon might well crumble under the scrutiny of his father.

"And you agree with this?" he spat, startling Haakon so much that Swein felt him jump beside him. Swein had heard enough.

"Everyone agrees with this father, apart from a handful of your most loyal followers. They wait for you at the coast, Finulf and Harth have led them there, swayed them to you. You can leave and never return. I'll escort you there myself to make sure you don't try and do anything foolish."

His father's gaze was still on Haakon and Swein was tempted to move into his line of sight, anything to stop him from staring at his brother. Not that Haakon was a weak man. Not at all. He ruled his own shipmen well and with far greater skill than their own father had ever done, but before their father he could quickly revert to a small child, terrified of his father's rages.

"If I refuse to go," his father said, his eyes glaring at Haakon still. At his side, Swein felt the air around him swirl, and then his brother was in front of him, his hand on his dagger at his side.

"If you refuse to go, father," his brother said, his voice strong and level, "I'll kill you myself, you bastard."

Swein felt his eyebrows rise in amazement at hearing those words ripped from his brother's mouth, but he knew they masked a lifetime that had fluctuated between abuse and total abandonment. Indifference had been the worst crime, far better to bear the marks of their father's anger than go from year to year without even a word or a look from him. The Old Gods had marked Swein, but Haakon hadn't even had that to cause their father's disinterest in him. No, he'd been perfectly formed; a good boy and still their father had hated him.

He reached out to touch his brother's arm and as he did he felt the quiver of Haakon's anger rushing through his body. No matter how he sounded, the anger that pulsed through him was intense.

"Even you?" their father said, his voice unable to mask his surprise at hearing Haakon speak as he did.

"Even I father the other son, the one you probably forget you ever gave life to," Haakon spoke smoothly, but those words burned the air when they left his mouth.

"My sons," their father said, trying a new tactic. He turned and looked at Swein. "My sons," he said again, his voice soft and oily. Swein shook his head in anger. Fuck the bastard. He wasn't about to let him try and diffuse the situation by appealing to any familial loyalty.

He pulled his dagger from his weapons belt, pleased when the noise of the metal leaving its sheath echoed throughout the preternaturally quiet room, jammed with the supporters of the brothers, the heat almost too much to endure. His father flinched at the sound and for the first time, Swein saw fear on his father's face. Good.

He leapt the short space between himself and his father, and before Harald could so much as call for his own weapon, Swein was stood beside him, his dagger at his throat, cutting deeply through his long, white beard with the dragon claw sharpened edge of his blade.

Harald looked at him, his eyes showing his worry and fear, and Swein stepped even closer and circled his head so that Harald's neck was completely exposed. How easy it would be just to hack through his fragile neck here and now. How easy and how very, very wrong it would be.

"Get up, slowly and carefully, I wouldn't want to cut you accidentally," he whispered into his father's ear, drinking in the smell of fear and sweat that emanated from him. "Walk towards the door and get on your damn horse and ride from here. Now." He shouted the last word, remembering how his father had employed the same technique against his own sons with great effect. Harald almost jumped to his feet in his desire to do as his son commanded. Swein noted that tactic for future reference. He'd always thought it had only worked because they'd been boys and his father a strong man. That didn't seem to be the case.

"Don't speak, just walk," Swein continued. The men of the warband were watching carefully. Everyone had instructions not to intervene. Harald, totally unaware of the actions planned against him, had no support, not anymore. Swein hadn't lied. His people, those who wished to stay with their king, were waiting for him at the coast. He'd managed to single each and every one of them out and have them removed from Hedeby without his father even noticing the dwindling number of men and women at his table.

Swein didn't care where they went as long as they never, ever came back to Denmark. He never wanted to see his father again.

From behind his head, he wasn't able to see his father's expression, but he was pleased to feel him rise and start to walk forward. He kept the blade at his throat, although he gave him room to move. He was far taller than his father, something else the old man had probably never realised. It was easy for him to hold his arm up and keep it steady. He'd spent days and days training to become a great warrior, and days and days more learning how to command and sail a ship. The muscles along the side of his arm bulged as he walked but he felt no pressure on his arm and knew that he wouldn't misstep and inadvertently kill his father and neither would his arm quiver under the strain and accidentally strike him.

He'd taken great pains to ensure that his father wouldn't die at his hand. He wasn't about to undo all his hard work.

Men who'd grown uncomfortable under his father's command, his sister's husband to name just one of them, had pledged their support provided Harald wasn't murdered in cold blood. Swein knew that in the coming year he would need all the support he could get as he consolidated his hold on the throne and he wasn't about to lose support by killing his father when he didn't need to.

No, his father was a defeated man, and without any bloodshed. That would make it even more difficult for his father to reconcile in his mind. A bloodless coup was still a coup.

At the door to the great hall, his father stumbled, and Swein imagined it was done on purpose. Expertly he held the dagger away from his father's throat while the old man regained his balance. He also placed his other arm on his father's shoulder, to steady him.

"Don't worry old man. I don't intend your death today," he spoke into his ear, and he felt his father grimace. He was right. His father had been trying to kill himself with his dagger. He imagined Harald had decided it was better to die in such a way that his son would be blamed than leave with nothing but a few old men and women in disgrace.

Outside it was a mild summer afternoon, with winter nipping

at its heels. His father stopped again, his head tilting towards the wooden church where his father lay buried.

"No you can't," Swein said. "You should have made your peace with your father years ago. Now mount your horse."

As he spoke a horse was led forward, his father's favourite beast and far too valuable to be allowed to leave the royal hall, but Swein knew if he didn't let his father take the animal he would complain loudly. It was a small thing to concede to have him gone as soon as possible.

His own horse was also ready for him to mount, and twenty of his men were milling around on their own horses. It would take them little time to reach the waiting ships. From there they'd follow his father until he made it to the open sea. Haakon would remain behind in Hedeby to ensure the smooth transition of power.

Swein had been tempted to send him with their father, but he knew Haakon wasn't quite as in control of his emotions as he pretended. Alone with their father, he might well kill him yet, and he couldn't let that happen, far better for him to perish in a winter sea storm than at the hands of either of his sons.

His father made a great show of mounting his horse, his movements intentionally slow, but Swein held his tongue. He had what he wanted. If his father wished to make a huge fool of himself, then he was entitled to do so.

Finally, and with a final nod towards Haakon, he grabbed the reins of his father's horse and forced the animal forward, against his father's commands. He didn't watch his father as he took his final look at his family home. He'd never see it again, but Swein would.

CHAPTER 3

Hedeby, Denmark
AD986

He crashed through the closed doorway of his hall. His face was set against the terrible weather that had beset his journey home after seeing his father off. Since his father's ship had sailed out of sight, accompanied by three other vessels packed with his father's possessions and his followers, the weather had turned decidedly wintry, and he'd cursed his father all the way back to his home. His constant delaying tactics had turned the mission to escort him from his lands from a pleasant late summer jaunt, into a race against the coming winter storms.

If only Harald had travelled with more haste, then he'd have been home and within his warm bed days ago. Then he wouldn't have much cared if enough snow had fallen from the sky to make journeys impossible for the remainder of the year. It would have allowed him time to luxuriate in his bloodless coup against his father, given him time to enjoy being a king before any hard decisions were forced upon him.

No matter what else they said about him when men wrote down their skewed histories in years to come, no doubt in the hand of some Christian monk who never stepped foot outside the sanctuary of his monastery, they'd not be able to stain his reputation with false stories of how he'd murdered his own father and taken his kingdom. No, he'd worked hard to ensure that could never happen. He'd taken his father's kingdom because he ruled it too closely, too tightly, and men couldn't breathe with him as their king and because he was a better ruler, a wiser man for all that he was half his age. He'd taken it because his father's hold on the loyalty of his men had been so weak that it had been accomplished with almost no hardship at all.

He shrugged free from his great fur-lined cloak, careful to ensure the rain only pooled near the door and not in the middle of the hall. He shook the weather from his head and turned expectantly to look for his brother. He knew Haakon would have consolidated their position while he'd been away. He'd given him little else to do because he was aware that it needed to be him who ensured their father left the land of the Danes once and for all. He loved his brother, but his father would have swayed him because Haakon had always been so desperate for a show of love from his father. Any show of love would have done it, and on the journey to the sea his father would have realised that, and Swein would have been met with his father's return to Hedeby.

As the welcome heat of the fires burning at the centre of the room swept over him, and his cloak was taken by one of his father's many servants, now his own, his eyes sought out and found his brother. He was speaking with another at the front of the hall. His tense posture made it clear that whoever it was wasn't a welcome guest. Swein knew a moment of panic. Who was this man? He looked like a Danish man, but he also looked to be a powerful man, arm rings running almost all the way up his arms to his shoulders and yet Swein did not know whom he was.

Striding forward to interject in the conversation, he was waylaid by his youngest sister, her face concerned and excited in equal measure. She looked much like he remembered their mother, only filled with more life. He knew men craved her beauty but for now, she was too valuable to be handed over to another man in marriage.

"Brother," she said, her voice low and confidential. "I take it you had great success," her bright eyes were keen to hear that their father had gone. Beside her, his father's second wife stepped close as well. She was just as eager to hear the news. Swein thought once more it was a shame he couldn't take her as his wife, only as his partner in bed. She was a truly beautiful woman with long luscious blond hair, braided elaborately around her head, and an enticing figure, with full breasts and a flat stomach many women were envious of. But he knew she'd give anything to curve with the extra weight of a baby. Pity it was never to be the case.

"Yes, he's gone. He made an arse of himself, but in the end, he left, as we knew he would. The sea was rolling, torrid and grey as he set off towards the lands of his allies."

"You think the sea will take him?" his sister asked eagerly, and he grinned at her, caught up in her excitement and forgetting all about the stranger in their midst.

"We can hope, but his Christian God might protect him so that he can go and spread the word of Christianity."

Gytha laughed at that, her head thrown back. His sister always surprised him. For so many years he'd thought her a fragile gem to be protected. He'd been both right and wrong. She was made of the hardest diamond he'd ever encountered.

He also met the eyes of Thora, and she nodded with pleasure. She'd not been the easiest to convince that his father needed to leave the land of the Danes, but once he'd converted her to his way of thinking, she'd been a willing accomplice, both in and out of his bed.

Gytha nodded towards Haakon then.

"That man, he came a few days ago, and Haakon has been keeping him company ever since. He says his name is Olaf and what he's come to offer you his support."

"Olaf who?" Swein asked his sister, but she shook her head.

"I don't know. Haakon has carried out your wishes too well. He's banished me from the front of the hall and so I don't know anything more about him."

"Has he been sleeping within the hall?" Swein asked. He was curious to see how friendly his brother had become with the stranger.

"Yes, but with all of Haakon's guard in attendance. He's had them all taking guard duties. I don't know if Olaf's even realised. If he has, he's been remarkably calm about it all. He only has ten men with him."

Swein took in the view of the man at the front of his hall as he tried to decide just which Olaf this might be. There were far too many Olaf's currently plying their trade as kings, jarls and vikings and if he didn't know whom his father or his mother was, it was almost impossible to determine who he was and what he wanted within his hall. He'd heard no rumours of a new warlord, but then, he'd been caught up in usurping his father's kingship and hadn't been concerned with external forced for some time.

He felt certain that he hadn't come to lay claim to his kingship. If he had, he'd have brought a vast army and not just a spattering of his men.

Haakon had noted his arrival but his guest had not. Swein realised he had a choice; he could slip in beside his brother and just join the conversation, as though he was another warrior, or he could introduce himself. He wavered between the two options and then chose the latter. He had nothing to hide, and he imagined that Olaf had come to speak with the King of Denmark, no one else.

"Brother," he called to Haakon, making it clear that his intention was to be introduced as the king, as he walked towards the front of the hall. His brother grinned, just as their younger sister had on seeing him, and strode towards him, knocking his stool over in his haste to stand. Haakon grasped him tightly in his arms as he embraced him.

"Tell me the old bastard's gone?" he said, and Swein stepped back to look at him. Already his brother looked far better than ever before in his life. The knowledge that he'd no longer be subject to their father's indifference had lifted him from shadows and bathed him in light. Swein idly wondered if he looked just as changed, or if he would once he was rested from his journey and no longer suffering from an extended journey outside in the chill air.

"I assure you he's gone. But still, I've left a ship to watch the mouth of the river and to prevent his return if he should consider one. He's gone, brother. We'll never see him again."

He stepped back from his brother then and looked meaningfully at the other man. He was younger than them but only by a few short years. He carried himself easily despite his great bulk, smothered in great furs and with his treasures on display. He was a warrior and probably a ship's captain as well.

"Swein, this is Olaf, son of Tryggve, king of Viken."

Swein narrowed his eyes as he looked at Olaf. After all, he had heard tales of him, about his exile and birth after his father's death. He wondered what he was doing seeking him out.

"I always wanted a father," Olaf said, interjecting in the conversation without acknowledging his introduction by Haakon. "It appears as though I might well have been mistaken in wanting one." His voice was warm and welcoming, a pleasant change from the chill of the outside.

Swein felt his lips quirk at the unusual opening line, although his brother stiffened at the words.

"Fathers can be difficult to manage," Swein simply replied, making himself comfortable at the table where Haakon's men moved aside to let him sit. He was pleased to note that they'd not left Haakon alone with Olaf but had been watching and listening. At his side, Dryi stood, attentively, despite the fact that on the journey home he'd announced his plans to sleep for a week when they made it back. He helped himself to a jug and drinking horn. He splashed the fluid into the horn and raised it at his brother, and behind him, at his sister and his lover. He indicated that Dryi should join him, but he declined, standing stiffly behind his new king.

"They don't always die when you want them to, and neither do they do as they're told," Swein finally replied, having considered how best to answer the question. He supposed other men might well ask him similar questions in the future. It was best to be as politic as possible when he spoke about taking his father's kingdom.

Olaf nodded his head as he considered those words.

"So really I'm the luckier man because my father was killed before my birth."

"You were, but not so anymore. My father is gone, and he won't be returning. I'm king of these lands now."

"Ah," Olaf said, "I think you might be a little presumptuous in your statement, and that's why I'm here." He still spoke languidly, as though they discussed women or the weather, but Swein could feel his heart beat quickening. What did this man know? What had he heard? He thought quickly. Who had he forgotten to collude with when he went about usurping his father? He'd had contact with the King of Norway, and he'd ensured that the Jomsvikings were still licking their wounds from their most recent defeat against the Norwegian King, Haaken. Was there some new force he was unaware of? Other than Olaf.

Olaf waved his hand then.

"Not that it is an immediate concern. Oh no. Don't fret so King Swein. It's just a little something I think you might need some help with come the raiding season next year when men deem it safe to leave their safe harbours."

Swein was torn, to hear himself called King was a great thing, the first time it had yet happened to him, and yet this Olaf seemed to promise war in his future, and he'd worked hard to ensure the transition would be smooth. He knew he was skilled enough to win any battle, to combat any attempt to seize his throne, but now Olaf was making him reconsider his closely held personal belief. He didn't want to be as blind as his father had been. He needed to know if others were going to move against him and he also needed to appear strong.

"And what do you propose to do about this threat?" Swein asked with interest. In truth, he was annoyed with himself that he needed to beg for the information.

Now Olaf looked keen, his indifference vanishing from his face.

"I want to ally with you, help you keep your country whole, make a name for myself raiding far and wide towards the eastern land. And then, well then I want your help to gain back my kingdom, become your ally, or your vassal, although I think I'll make a far better ally than a vassal. I'm not the easiest of men to command."

Swein considered the words. Olaf didn't seem to be offering him anything and would surely demand much in return for his support. If he did gain his land back, the birthright of his father, it seemed clear that he was already hinting that he wouldn't pay taxes to the man who'd helped him gain his kingdom.

"How many ships do you have?" he asked. He didn't see much point in continuing the conversation. The man was a displaced prince. He had nothing and wanted to use Swein to grow his reputation and renown. Swein had enough to contend with at the moment.

But a smile fleetingly shot across Olaf's face, and Swein wondered what was so funny. His brother was trying to tell him something with his expansive eyes, but Swein was deaf to it all. What had he said to make Olaf smirk?

"Just twenty my Lord Swein," he said, his words dropping like stones into a pool and sending ripples crashing to the edges and overflowing onto good pasture.

Swein barely stopped himself from choking on the mead he was in the process of swigging nonchalantly. Twenty, how could the man have twenty ships? That could mean he had at least a thousand men who called him their Lord, if not more. Swein had no idea how large the man's ships were.

"You see, I'm not just a displaced prince. I had a good wife who brought me much power and wealth and men flocked to me. Each of my ships can carry at least sixty men."

Swein was stunned and took the time to reconsider Olaf's offer. He was a man it was probably best to remain on good terms with. With a fighting force of well over a thousand men, if he had sixty men in each of his ships, he would be difficult to defeat if he decided to claim any part of Denmark for himself. Swein had his men, an army of men at the Trelleborg forts his father had built, but to have so many men concentrated in one place and mobile as well was a testament to Olaf's power and organisational skills.

Olaf's attention had wandered, either intentionally or not, but it gave Swein time to make eye contact with his brother. Haakon was nodding at him as though to confirm what Olaf had said, his head bobbing one too many times with the quantity of mead he'd drunk. It would have been comical if Swein hadn't been so busy thinking about this latest development.

The men who plied the seas between Norway, Sweden and Denmark, and now even further afield to Greenland, if the rumours were to be believed, were a fiercely stubborn and independent breed. Making alliances was almost counter-productive because no sooner had one alliance been agreed upon than another jarl was trying to undermine it. His father had learnt this to his detriment, trying to force his thoughts and beliefs on men who already knew their own minds and had the weapons to enforce their independence.

"Where are your men now?" Swein finally thought to ask, trying to keep the concern from his voice. He'd barely paid any attention when he'd ridden through the sheeting rain to his hall, desperate to be home and in the dry. It was just possible that over a thousand men were encamped around his hall and he'd not even noticed through the heavy clouds and hard-hitting rain.

"I left them some distance from here. I didn't wish to cause any alarm when I only come to eat and speak, and talk of raiding, not to make war." Olaf's answer was intentionally vague, and Swein felt Dryi stir behind him and then move away. He would return with a reply.

He raised his drinking horn to Swein and Swein unconsciously raised his own, an acceptance of the man's power and in thanks for his forethought. He was thinking frantically. How could he best remain on good terms with the warrior without committing to helping him in any way? And how could he gain the knowledge he held? He needed to know if anyone planned on rising against him. His father had spent much of his life fighting off attackers, if not the men from the German lands he shared a land border with, then the men of Norway and Sweden and their vast fleets, the seas no impediment to determined men.

"Where do you plan to raid?" he finally asked, having searched his mind for as benign a question as possible.

"I thought I'd try my luck in England. I've heard great tales of the riches the country has, and I think I'd like to go somewhere that has gold and silver in as much abundance as we have water and snow."

England. Swein thought that sounded like an excellent idea. He'd not yet been to England himself, but men within his war-bands and ship army had, and he knew that Olaf was correct. England was wealthy and exposed in equal measure.

"I will raid with you," Swein announced. He could see no other way of untangling himself from the man who'd decided he wanted to be his ally. He didn't want him in Denmark, and he didn't want his army camped on his borders.

"In the summer?" Olaf asked with arched eyebrows and amusement in his eyes.

"Hopefully, it will depend on events in Denmark first."

"Of course, of course. If you don't wish to raid England next year I'll go somewhere else, and we can attack the year after, or the year after, provided we do raid," he finished the conversation with a thread of menace running through his friendly voice.

"We will raid, yes. And you will tell me of the men who threaten my rule."

"I will, soon, but first we must discuss how many men you have, King Swein, and where you usually raid."

Swein felt his equilibrium return then. He wondered just how much Olaf knew about his father's building projects, his military projects.

"I will show you where my men live. It's a journey from here. I only keep my household guard here, not my warriors."

Olaf considered that, his eyes flickering between Haakon and Swein. Swein was pleased. It was evident that Haakon had managed to keep the conversation away from important matters of state. He would have to remember to thank him later.

His brother needed to be rewarded for his support of his kingship. He could have stood against their father himself, but he'd decided to support Swein. Swein needed to remember that. He needed to value his brother in ways that their father never had.

"Stay, be my guest for a few nights and then I'll show you where my warriors live."

Olaf glanced at a group of men sat before the fire. Swein recognised none of them and quickly realised they must be the men who'd come to support Olaf in his bid to make an alliance. He watched them with interest.

They seemed much the same as any other warriors he'd ever seen, but, well, there was a calm assurance about them that surprised him in a hall full of possible enemies. They were as arrogant as his father had been or they were simply skilled warriors, men who trusted their weapons and their fighting abilities more than they did each other.

He suddenly appreciated that the lessons he'd learned from watching his father might not be the only ones he needed to learn to be a successful king.

"Introduce me to your men?" he asked Olaf and the younger man grinned.

"Why my Lord, so that you can steal them? I don't think so."

Swein had the words of denial on his lips, but Olaf surprised him once more by laughing.

"I jest my Lord. If I was dead and gone, even then you might struggle to entice my men from my allegiance. I only have the most loyal of men, the truest to me. Any who only 'thinks' he wants to be one of my warriors and ship-men aren't welcome." As he spoke, he beckoned for one of the largest men Swein had ever seen to join them at the front of the hall.

He ambled towards his Lord, his intent clear and yet it was obvious he came only because he wanted to and not because he was commanded to. His eyes flashed with the same amusement that seemed to infect everything that Olaf said and did.

"This my Lord Swein is Axe. A strange name for a man but we have called it him for so long none can remember his real name. It is apt all the same."

Swein reached out to grasp the man's arm in greeting, steeling himself for the great weight he knew was about to be pressed on his own arm in retaliation for the welcome. He wasn't disappointed. Axe had a hand twice as large as his own and his fingers, when they squeezed, almost turned his hand to a tingling mass.

"King Swein," the man bellowed, his voice reaching out to touch every nook and cranny within the hall.

"Axe, it's my pleasure to meet you."

Axe's eyes glittered with amusement at the warm greeting from a king.

"It's my pleasure to be drinking such fine mead and food. Olaf only serves wet fish and cold water."

Olaf rolled his eyes at Axe's words and shook his head to deny them. Swein was taken aback. It was obvious that Olaf was the leader of the war band, and yet he was happy for his men to speak openly about his lack.

"Axe loves his food and complains about every meal I've served since we left Wendland. He forgets that it's not as easy to cook on a ship far out to sea and that its hard to serve beef because cows don't, in my learned opinion, tend to swim to their deaths."

Haakon was laughing drunkenly at the interplay between the two men, his relief that his older brother was back to deal with the situation evident in his amusement.

"Sit down and send Horic here. He knows how to speak before a king," Olaf commanded dryly, and Axe inclined his head to Swein and his brother and slunk back to his seat beside the fire.

The next man who walked towards Swein was certainly more a man than a giant. He was tall and well built, but Swein knew that if they shared an arm-clasp of friendship, he'd still be able to use his fingers afterwards. He'd spent the time listening to the interplay between Olaf and Axe with his hand under the table, flexing it to get some feeling back into it.

"My Lord Swein, this is Horic. A man with a brain as well as the fighting skills of Odin."

Horic offered a wry smile to Swein as he reached to grasp his arm.

"Well met King Swein. You have a grand hall here," he offered, and Swein relaxed around the man. It was more than obvious that he understood how to offer polite words to those in positions of power.

"Well met Horic. You come from Wendland where Olaf lived?" Swein asked, trying to piece together as much as he could about the men in his hall.

"No my Lord, I'm a Dane, but I travelled to Wendland when I heard of Olaf's renown from another raider."

"You've been with him for many years?" he asked, surprised that Olaf's fame had travelled as far as Denmark and that he'd never heard of him.

"Six years my Lord. No more. My wife and family are still here. I spend the winters with them."

Swein was thinking quickly. Here was a man he imagined he could tempt to live within one of his fortresses, but he wasn't about to make himself an enemy by stealing away one of Olaf's most respected warriors. Swein harboured the thought that Olaf had chosen these two men on purpose; the thug of a warrior and the most refined man with a family to provide for. He thought Olaf was testing him but to what end he didn't yet know. He appeared open and honest when he spoke, but he had secrets that he wasn't sharing.

A touch on his shoulder and he turned to see the smile of his younger sister. She was watching Olaf with far too much interest.

"Brother," she whispered, "you should speak to your people. Many are concerned that Harald may not be gone."

He berated himself then. That had been his intention all along, but the arrival of Olaf and his men had almost made him forget he was only newly come to the kingdom.

"My thanks, sister, I will," Swein said as he stood to turn and look at the mass of people who were now squeezed within the hall at Hedeby.

He saw all the men and women who'd supported him and a crushing sense of burden swept over him. It was one thing to watch his father and hate his every breath, every action. It was quite another to take his place and assume his responsibilities.

He took a deep breath and forced a smile to his face. Beside him

30

his brother stood, showing his full support for his brother, their sister on his other side and his father's estranged wife hovering near the back of their small group. Swein felt emboldened by the support he was receiving.

"My people," he began and smiled when a wave of cheers rippled through the audience. "I stand before you as your King, supported by my brother and my sister." He gestured towards Gytha who flushed prettily at the praise. "And Thora as well," he made no allusion to her position as the old King's wife. There was no need. "Together we will do great things." Again cheers rang out and then he looked to Olaf and an idea began to take form in his mind.

"And already we have allies who seek our strength and our power. Olaf of Wendland sits here with me and together we've decided to raid in the summer season." Huge cheers erupted from the men and women then, and Swein turned to Olaf with a questioning expression on his face. Olaf raised his drinking horn at the official recognition of his mission to Swein, and his men joined in the raucous calls for treasure and slaves.

"Tonight we'll feast together," he finished before raising his fist in victory and grinning at the people assembled before him. He needed to show them his enjoyment at the moment. It wouldn't do if they saw his newly formed doubts.

He turned back to Olaf and gestured that he was going outside. Olaf nodded his head to show he understood and followed him, indicating that his men should stay where they were. Axe didn't look happy about it, but Swein ignored that moment of distrust. Olaf would be a fool if his men weren't trained to think of treachery at every door.

Outside the hall, the rain continued to pour down, and Swein suddenly thought it wasn't such a good idea, but he needed to speak to Olaf alone.

He grabbed his cloak and stepped outside into the pooling puddles and grey sky, prematurely dark. He shivered a little. He'd be pleased to be back beside his fire, but first, he needed to ensure that Olaf was truly his ally and not just trying his luck.

"Not the most pleasant of days," Olaf commented as he joined him near to the bare ground where the horses were stabled in drier weather.

"Not at all. And not the sort of day you expect to find a stranger at your table," Swein commented sourly. He was annoyed by Olaf's intrusion on what should have been his time of ultimate triumph.

Olaf's good cheer didn't abate.

"I heard things. I wanted to take full advantage of any slight head start I might have on others, especially those from the land of my birth."

Swein absorbed the information. It was as he'd suspected. His father had supported the man who'd ultimately killed Olaf's father, and Olaf, a widower now, wanted to ensure that if he made a play for his ancestral kingdom, Swein wouldn't be a hindrance to his plans.

"You hoped to take advantage of my fledgeling reign?" he pressed.

Olaf shrugged his shoulders, a movement that made more noise than it should because of the exquisite jewels and metals that adorned his clothing.

"You can try and look for conspiracy where there is none," he quietly said, "or you can accept your good fortune. It's not a big issue for me."

Swein's gaze was riveted on where an upturned water barrel was quickly filling. Soon it would overflow, he counted the raindrops in his head, thinking to himself that by the time he reached a hundred, water would be pooling over the water barrel. The distraction worked to clear his mind, to think about what he needed to do.

"I will be your ally, and you will be mine, but only for so long as it's beneficial to me. I will not fight your battles, and I will not help you claim back your kingdom when you've made it clear you will pay no taxes to me or be my subordinate."

Olaf fixed him with a firm stare, his eyes sparkling with suppressed anger. Swein was surprised it had taken so long for Olaf's good spirits to depart but pleased that he'd finally managed to ruffle the man. It had taken long enough.

"As you will King Swein. And I assure you. I'll not help you hold your kingdom. We'll be raiding partners, nothing more."

With that, Olaf turned and headed back inside the hall.

Swein watched him go with no satisfaction and then he remembered.

"Who's my enemy?" he called to the retreating back of the man. Olaf stopped and turned slowly, a grin of malice on his face.

"Everyone is your enemy now, King Swein." He said nothing further but walked inside the warmth of the great hall.

Swein realised he'd either just made his first ally or his first enemy as king of Denmark. Only time would show him the outcome of his actions.

He breathed heavily.

So, this was what it meant to be a king.

He could almost enjoy it if only it weren't so bloody wet.

CHAPTER 4

Aggersborg, Denmark
Summer AD994

Swein watched the men and their ships beaching on the gentle slope with a jaundiced eye. He'd heard many, many things about Olaf since their first meeting seven years ago. He imagined that some of them were blown vastly out of proportion, or so he hoped.

Olaf Tryggvason had proved to be a cunning warrior, and he and his men ate well and raided far and wide. Rumours of their exploits often entertained Swein and his men through the dark times of the year. Olaf had so far avoided any land that Swein might hold a claim to, but Swein knew that sooner or later Olaf was going to do something that would upset him. Olaf was too powerful to be ignored, and the Jarls and would-be Jarls of the kingdoms that surrounded Swein's own found him too tempting a pawn to ignore. Olaf could bring great victory and also great defeat if he could be cajoled to join with them.

Olaf's refusal to engage in the vast battle between the Jomsvikings and Haaken, his father's repudiated ally, that had erupted at the same time he was removing his father from power, had led to the defeat of the Jomsvikings and to Haaken becoming over mighty in his lands in Norway. Swein had always respected Haaken's defiance against his father. It had been one of the many events that had revealed to Swein his father's weaknesses. His father couldn't see that in trying to force Christianity on Haaken, a man who staunchly believed in the old Gods, that all he was doing was losing himself an ally. And an ally a who'd stood with him for many, many years. His father's loss had been Haaken's gain, and Olaf's failure to ally with the Jomsvikings had also worked to Haaken's advantage.

Swein hoped that by raiding England together with Olaf, he'd distract the man and his ship-army enough that they'd turn their eyes elsewhere, not towards Denmark and hopefully, not towards the land he coveted in Norway either.

Olaf was married once more, to a wife who held great riches, although not a great beauty and he had no need to raid, but he and his men had a streak in them that demanded their yearly raiding parties. The rumours of England's weak king and reliable coinage system were, Swein assumed, what currently drove them. And something else as well, but Swein wasn't sure whether it was the need to claim some small piece of England for himself, or whether Olaf still aspired to the lands of Norway he felt were his birthright and was prepared to do anything to facilitate his acquisition of them.

Swein hoped to find out and stop Olaf from encroaching on the land of his other allies and putting him in an awkward predicament. He didn't want Olaf as an enemy, not at all and if he had to make a choice between him and those who shared land or sea borders with him, Swein hazarded a guess that Olaf would be his ally of strength, if not of choice.

He'd been a king for long years now, and in that time he'd made many alliances, and watched many of them fall by the wayside. He had children of his own, two boys, Harald named for his father, his attempts to cast someone with the name into a better man, and Cnut named for his wife's father. Swein hoped he was a kinder father than his own had ever been, but the children were still almost too young to be interesting.

Swein wanted sons to train with an axe and a seax, not children more interested in playing hide and seek. Both boys held the spark of great promise provided they grew to manhood and learned the ways of a king and his warband, a king and his people and perhaps more importantly, a king and the faith of the people he ruled. He tried to love his sons equally, to give them the same in everything, but it wasn't always easy to accomplish. Cnut was precocious and showed the most spark, but Harald was staid. Harald would happily spend his life counting tree trunks and reinforcing the Trelleborg forts, Cnut would not. That was already clear to see.

The most important lesson for the boys to learn would be that which instinctively told whether a man was your friend or your enemy. Swein knew he still struggled with that part of his kingship. He chose never to trust and that caused almost as many problems as trusting too easily. He'd offended many men and women with his cautious ways.

Swein watched Olaf jump from the front of his mighty ship, Long Serpent, and stride towards him, a wide grin of welcome on his wind-weathered face. Olaf carried his years well. He moved with the fluidity of the rolling sea and Swein almost felt a moment of nausea as he watched the man. Swein liked the sea but was always pleased to touch dry land and feel the ground firm beneath his feet.

Long Serpent was a massive craft, dwarfing all those that sat awaiting loading with men and supplies. Swein felt a rumble of jealously. He'd prefer a ship like that to his carefully ordered forts.

The ships-head held a long curving tongue, painted bright red, and its malice easy to interpret. The rest of the serpent was black as night with shining eyes that seemed to watch his every move. Swein shivered a little as he gazed at it. Olaf had chosen his symbol well.

Olaf was even more at ease with himself than he had been when they'd first met. He'd had a great victory already against the English king and his prize three years ago had been a vast treasure of ten thousand pounds, a sum so huge Swein struggled to comprehend what the men could have used it for. Swein hoped that the men had not all buried it in deep holes, to be forgotten about if they died on their next raiding expedition.

It would be a terrible waste if that were the case.

After Olaf's great success he'd turned once more to Swein and offered him the opportunity to raid with him. Given his significant achievements elsewhere, Swein knew he couldn't delay the inevitable any longer. He'd managed to postpone it for long enough as it was, always being beset by enemies he needed to subdue elsewhere, and Olaf had always been convivial enough to take no offence from the constant delays.

Since becoming king, Swein had spent only his winters in Denmark, the rest of the time he'd been raiding or warring with his enemies in Norway, Sweden and on the land borders with the reaching hands of those from the German lands who threatened to overwhelm the Danevirke again. Swein faced the same problems his father had, but he thought he dealt far more efficiently with them. He was more likely to have allies than enemies, despite his cautious approach to people and he needed to keep it that way.

Now Swein watched with interest as Olaf sized up the might of his fleet. Having been shocked by the vast numbers Olaf had been able to command when they'd first met, Swein had grown his quota of men, using both the fortresses built by his father and those that he'd had built himself.

It still amused him to think that he'd assumed his responsibilities as king would have been about high matters of state, laws, taxes and justice, not how many trees it took to reinforce one of the trelleborg forts. He and his brother often joked about their expertise in tree felling, his younger sister looking on with amusement.

His sister was to be married soon, and he'd miss her, but he also knew it was time she was married and gone from Denmark. Her husband was a devious man and one that Swein admired for his deceitful ways. However, he'd assured Swein that his feelings for his sister were genuine and that he was committed to making a good life with her.

Swein had smiled and nodded to hear his words before leaning over to him and whispering in his ear that he'd kill him if anything ever befell his sister.

Pallig had swallowed hard on hearing that. Swein hoped it made him reconsider just how important Gytha was to her elder brother. Pallig was a man of wealth and land in Denmark, but he needed to realise that the hand of the king's sister was something to be treasured and not something to hoard away as another possession.

Before them at the port closest to Aggersborg over sixty ships under the command of Swein were being outfitted for war. While Olaf now commanded thirty ships filled with men, and many of his ships were far larger than Swein's own, it meant that to all intents and purposes, Swein was the dominant force behind their proposed invasion of England.

Swein wanted to enjoy the moment, but as was so often the case, Olaf was giving little away. Olaf's good cheer must on occasion be tempered, but Swein had only ever broken through it that once, and never again. It was as though Olaf worked to be as affable as possible. It was a skill Swein knew he'd never master. His wife often told him that he wore too much of himself on his face. He couldn't deny her words. She wasn't the first to say so, and she wouldn't be the last either.

"Tell me of England," Swein said to Olaf when they'd greeted each other as cordially as they could. Olaf watched him with sharp eyes, and Swein felt as though all of his thoughts and worries were evident to Olaf without him even asking.

Still, he was curious to know what Olaf made of the place they planned on raiding. Olaf grinned wildly, as was usual, and paused for a long moment as he considered his words. Men rushed around them readying ships and moving supplies and yet somehow in the hustle and bustle both had been presented with drinking cups and plates of food as well as small wooden stools to rest on. Swein could have laughed at the absurdity of the situation, crafts of war spread before them while their commanders snacked on delicacies.

"She's not the easiest place to breach. She has many waterways and far too much coastline and the men who defend her know how to fight. I can see why they managed to prevent our ancestors from taking the whole island. But they have some flaws as well, the main one being honour. I can assure you that neither you nor I will ever suffer from that," Olaf continued, his voice filled with enjoyment.

Swein felt himself stiffen at the intended insult, but actually, Olaf had made a fair assessment of him. He wasn't a man of too much honour. There was no time for it, and after all, in the end, he'd been forced to kill his father when he'd tried to retake Denmark from him. That was not an honourable thing to have done, no matter how much his father had deserved to lose the kingdom.

"The warriors of England are well provisioned and have excellent skills," Olaf continued. "The trick is to attack in a number of locations very quickly. Then they don't seem to know where to go to prevent further skirmishes."

"Where do you plan on leading our men this time?"

"I think we should head for London, the greatest town in England, apart from Winchester which the king calls his home. London is situated on a great river, but inland. It'll take skill to get to London along the Thames and greater ability to escape with all our men and the riches we desire." Olaf spoke the words without fear. It was evident to Swein that he relished the coming altercation.

Swein thought about the wisdom of attacking somewhere so difficult. He thought they should perhaps try for somewhere less conspicuous, and somewhere it would be easier to achieve an escape.

"They store great wealth within London. There are many churches richly endowed with gold and silver. London would be a good place to start," Olaf continued, as though once more, he knew what Swein was thinking.

"Tell me of your last battle," Swein asked, to cover his unease, and Olaf turned to smirk at him.

"They let us slaughter them like pigs. It was all too easy in the end. They had this man; I heard his name was Ealdorman Byrhtnoth, we would call him a jarl, who commanded the troops. He made a rousing speech about driving us from their shores, and then he let us cross onto firm land because the tide was going out and the ground was marshy, and of course, we took advantage of his honourable intentions and slaughtered them all."

Olaf laughed at his memory of the battle, and Swein saw the death of men on his open face. Olaf was an affable man until he held a weapon against your throat. Swein realised that he was a very deadly ally, and would make a far more mortal enemy.

"No one escaped the battle?" Swein asked with interest. Rumours of the famous battle at Maldon had reached even his ears in Hedeby. It was intriguing to hear Olaf's version of events.

"No, I think perhaps one or two escaped, no more. If none had survived how would anyone know how lethal the battle was and fear another attack?" Olaf joked and Swein laughed along with him despite the sense of foreboding he felt.

Swein wanted to raid England for its wealth. He could see why Olaf thought it was all so easy, but he also worried that it might be too easy and that Olaf would gain more renown and wealth from the battle than he would. After all, he was a king; he was supposed to be able to subdue others, and he could negotiate with the English king as an equal. Olaf was only a very successful warrior, nothing more. Men would not expect him to make significant gains, not as they would Swein.

Olaf was far stronger than Swein had ever thought he'd become. Men flocked to his service, and they did so willingly. It was dangerous to have such a charismatic man answer to no one other than himself and his warriors, and perhaps his wife. Swein grinned at that. He's heard just as many rumours about Olaf's second wife as he had his raiding exploits.

"The English let their bishops speak on their behalf. It's a weakness that makes them too keen to find peaceful ends to every battle."

Swein wrenched his attention back to what Olaf was telling him.

"You didn't meet the king then?"

"No, not the king. He never seems to fight himself, but only sends men to act in his name. I think he's scared to fight, for all that he's a relative of King Alfred, the man who held England against our ancestors a century ago."

"Perhaps his mother was a weak woman," Swein opined consideringly, but Olaf was shaking his head.

"No, I've heard she's a woman of formidable character, a queen in her own right. I don't know what muddles the thinking of the English king, but I intend to take full advantage of it. While he lets others fight his battles for him, and makes others pay their way out of defeat, I'm more than happy to take advantage of his vulnerabilities."

"What others, who else do you have joining us?"

Swein had been thinking about this for some time. He knew that in the past Olaf had sought other allies.

"No one else for now. I thought, my Lord Swein, that over ninety ships full of shipmen were more than enough. I don't want to deprive England of all her wealth. Then they'll be no treasure to go back for in a few years time." Still, Olaf laughed. It was all a game to Olaf.

It was clear that Olaf had given the matter some thought, far more than Swein had. It made him realise the main difference between him and Olaf. Olaf still had a kingdom to claim. Swein held his very securely. It meant Olaf was filled with needs and wants. Swein sometimes thought he'd forgotten to strive for greater success. He wanted to be content in his homelands, but his men wanted riches and gold. They were far keener to journey to England than he was. Swein believed this attack was his duty, to show that he upheld the promises he gave; his men saw it only as an opportunistic attack.

Not that his success had been gained easily, not at all, but at first it had been achieved with little bloodshed and only his father's desire for greater vengeance had meant he'd had to confirm his kingship with blood.

"When will we sail?" Swein asked, turning his thoughts back to the here and now.

"As soon as the men are all provisioned. And Lord Swein?"

"Yes, Lord Olaf, what is it?"

"Are you taking your men from your trelleborg forts or are they staying to defend Denmark?" Olaf dropped the question into the conversation as though it was of little importance.

Swein almost answered without thinking, that yes, he was taking all his men with him, but something warned him to be less forthcoming. It seemed like an innocent question but perhaps it wasn't.

"No, only from Aggersborg. The men from the other trelleborg forts will remain here."

Swein was sure Olaf knew he was lying, but he'd been struck by the question and couldn't shake the thought that Olaf was perhaps being paid by one of his enemies to tempt him away from Denmark so that another could attack it in his absence.

That was another of his problems. Swein tended to see conspiracy where perhaps none existed. Not that he'd ever acted irrationally. No, but his ease with taking the kingdom from his father had warned him that other men might be just as successful against him should they try their luck.

Swein walked away from Olaf, his thoughts busy, and he beckoned for his brother to join him.

"Haakon, I want you to sail out amongst the ships. Tell the men from the trelleborg forts other than Aggersborg to return home and guard Denmark in my absence. You must stay behind as well. I fear Olaf has something planned for when we're not here."

Haakon's eyes strayed to the ships in the busy little harbour as Swein spoke.

"He doesn't want Denmark?" Haakon said, more as though he was convincing himself than he was convinced of the answer.

"No, he doesn't. But that doesn't mean that the king of Norway or Sweden doesn't, or even the men from the mainland beyond the Danevirke."

"I should go with Olaf," Haakon immediately said, "you should stay at home."

"No, I can't. If I remain behind, Olaf will alert whoever it is and then we'll never know who means us harm. You must stay and defend the people and the land if you can, find out who means us ill."

"But brother, I wished to see England."

"I know Haakon, and soon, soon I'll let you go. Perhaps next year."

Haakon looked bitterly disappointed, and Swein almost reconsidered. But he was right to command as he had. Haakon would have more support at home than he would amongst Olaf and his men. If they fought the English king's men and tried to make a treaty with them, Olaf wouldn't accord Haakon anywhere near as much respect as he would if Swein himself was there. Haakon was the brother of the king, not the king. It would make a huge difference, and once agreement had been reached on everything, it would be almost impossible for Swein to gain any retribution if they settled matters to the detriment of Denmark.

"You'll govern for me instead. You'll piss my wife off," Swein said it with a hint of a smile that widened when Haakon groaned dramatically.

"Don't," he started to say but Swein held his hand up to stop his words.

"You'll have to," Swein simply said. "I'm sure you can get Gytha to intervene on your behalf. She's not an unreasonable woman," he finished a little lamely under the intense scrutiny of Haakon's gaze.

"I'll remind you of that the next time you complain about her."

Swein slapped his brother on the back, as much of an apology as he was going to get. He'd just tasked his brother with removing his wife from ruling while they went raiding. She'd be angry and outraged. There was no denying that. Swein almost wished he could be there to see it. Then he thought better of it. Hopefully by the time he returned home she'd have forgiven him. Perhaps.

The sea voyage towards England was accomplished with little fuss, the many ships staying within sight of each other as the sea remained reasonably calm. Swein watched the seascape with interest. He'd never travelled towards England before. He'd been to Shetland and Orkney when his father still ruled but never before had he sailed directly to England.

Olaf was filled with stories of its wealth and its lush green fields, bursting with healthy cattle and sheep, but Swein craved the renown he hoped to achieve almost as much as he did the thought of the wealth they'd acquire.

Swein allowed his ship's captain to direct the ship for the four-day journey and only as the coastline came into view did he even consider taking over from him.

The cliffs and beaches seemed similar to Denmark, Norway and Sweden and the sea was bitingly cold. Olaf made a point of directing them inland at a set point and pointing to a small island and an even smaller fortress a little way further south. It's wooden ramparts visible in the bright sunshine. It looked like an inviting place.

"Bamburgh," Olaf called to Swein, having maneuvered his ship so that it was level with his own.

Swein mulled the name over in his head, he'd heard of it but couldn't think why.

"And their Holy Island as well," Olaf also shouted to him, pointing at the original point of interest. Now that, at least, he knew. The tales of his ancestors attacking the island that had become England were legendary. Any warrior who hoped to win wide renown wished they'd had a mighty warrior from those early wars within his family's pedigree.

Swein could understand why. Even now the name of a powerful warrior who'd made his fortune in Mercia or Northumbria aroused respect. Most seemed to forget that many of the men had either died or settled in the land known as the Danelaw, a vast swathe of land more heavily occupied by the first Viking raiders than any other within England. Even now Swein knew that it held firmly to the laws of Denmark and travellers from the Danelaw were as happy within Denmark as they were in England.

It was almost as though those occupants were waiting for someone from Denmark to come and rule them. That almost filled Swein with excitement.

If they were to find any allies within the island, it was to the

Danelaw that they needed to go, but Olaf had different ideas.

"London," Olaf called, after the ships had bobbed on the water for a sufficient length of time for Swein to actually understand the openness of their Holy Island and the highly logical location of the fortress of Bamburgh. They watched people watching them from the ramparts, smoke from the cook fires swirling lazily into the cloudless sky, but neither side made any move to attack the other.

"Why London? Why not here?" Swein called back across the expanse of dark sea that separated their ships. They'd discussed this at length before they'd left his kingdom, but Swein wanted to reassure himself that they were acting in the best interests of their combined desires and not because Olaf wished to lead him into danger.

"There are too few people here Swein. Trust me. Their wealth is all in cattle and sheep, if we want coin we need to go somewhere with more people."

Swein knew that Olaf spoke the truth, and yet he had a sudden inkling that he'd like to at least place a foot on the glistening white sand that encircled Bamburgh. It looked enticing and welcoming in the bright sunshine of the late summer's day. More a place to rest and relax than one to shed blood and end lives. It was only under duress that he let Olaf steer the flotilla away from the coastline. Maybe one day he'd come back and explore the area further. One day.

CHAPTER 5
London
AD994

T he river stretched far and wide all around the fleet. Even with over ninety ships, the combined force felt too small on the vast river. Swein, rather than feeling sure of himself, felt a tiny prickle of fear and doubt when he watched the mouth of the river open up before them.

Olaf was filled with good cheer, making a rousing speech to the assembled ships as they made the turn to follow the river inland. Swein had felt emboldened by the speech himself, but as the vast fleet was funneled closer and closer together by the lessening of the sides of the river, he began to doubt the wisdom of the enterprise.

It was possible that they were being watched and that the English already knew they were here and that they were waiting around the next bend in the river to attack, a string of ships stretched across the river to stop their advance. Despite Olaf's assurances that the English would only respond to an attack on land and that they'd never actively seek one with men in fast ships, Swein was unconvinced. There was always a first time. Always.

Slowly, the banks of the river became more and more populated as they rowed steadily onwards. Cows and sheep gazed at the men as they passed and Swein knew that soon someone would send word to the local Jarl and that he would have no choice but to race out and meet their attack, perhaps stop it before it had even begun.

Olaf said that any defence the English mounted would be derisory. Swein hoped he was right. He had nearly two thousand men with him on the ships. He wanted to go back with each and every one of them, and he certainly wanted to ensure that his priceless ships made it back to his land. Perhaps not as valuable to men who had land to farm and til, the ships made Swein and his warriors able to respond quickly to any attack and to ensure that the exposed coastlines of his people were protected from any who tried to erupt from the Baltic Sea and take what wasn't there's. They'd been used in a number of sea battles already, and they'd be needed in the future, Swein was sure of it.

Olaf led the way along the mighty River Thames, his optimism floating on the gentle breeze and Swein watched him almost jealously. Olaf had impressed him when they'd first met, just after he'd claimed the throne from his father. Now, Olaf more than impressed him. He scared him, and Swein didn't like to be fearful of any man. Not since his father's rages had he allowed himself to be afraid before another man. He didn't want Olaf to know that he was awed by his easy nature and his prowess in battle, not to mention jealous of his huge success.

Men followed Olaf because he promised what they wanted. Swein had always known that men wanted a leader who could pledge and bring to fruition those promises. He'd always tried to do just that, but now he felt as though his efforts had been ineffectual.

Dryi joined him at the front of the ship, his head swivelling from side to side as he absorbed everything he could see.

"This land is richer than even our own," he said, awe lacing his words. Swein knew he was correct to think so.

"And more exposed as well," he added, hoping to make Dryi say something less complimentary.

"The stories of the riches of England weren't exaggerated, not at all, but I think Olaf sees only success and not the possibility of failure. You need to watch him carefully."

Dryi's thoughts were exactly what Swein needed to hear and at that moment his doubts turned themselves around. He was no Olaf, but he was Swein, King of the Danes. He'd claimed his throne on a tide of popularity, in stark contrast to his father's grudgingly given support and men still looked to him favourably. In the years since he'd been forced to meet and kill his father when he'd tried to reclaim the throne, he'd engaged many men in battle and kept the land of the Danes whole against many attacks from others who thought they would make a better king.

His warriors admired him, albeit in a very different way to Olaf. But he had more to give his men. He had land and wealth, the promise of a settled life with their family either within the Trelleborg forts or without. Olaf simply had the wealth.

He and Olaf had held a brief council of war before Olaf's inspiring speech at the mouth of the Thames. They'd formulated some ideas depending on how easy or difficult it proved to be to breach the defences of London.

Olaf was adamant it would be easy. He had, amongst his men, a number who had sailed up and down the great Thames as guards on board trading ships. He said he knew that the walls and ditches had been breached so many times that it would be easy to slide inside the town.

Swein had heard the opposite from his men. They said the walls stood taller than three men and almost as deep and that the ditches had been repaired in recent years because of the increasing unrest on the coastline. Olaf had given little thought to the attack. Swein had demanded that they make decisions now that would prevent misunderstandings later.

Olaf had agreed with his usual good cheer and Swein had felt mollified knowing that he'd acted decisively for the first time on their voyage. He'd also made a further choice that he didn't share with Olaf and that was to leave five of his ships sheltering at the mouth of the Thames.

If there were a counter-attack, as unlikely as Olaf thought it would be, he wanted to be assured of escaping the confining river and of knowing that they would not be prevented from shooting out of the Thames and dashing for freedom by a hastily scrambled English fleet that blocked the way. Unlike his homeland, bisected by waterways, often exposed to the sea and consisting of many small islands, he'd been told that even this enormous river finally ran dry long before they would find freedom on the far side of England.

The five ships had slipped slowly out of sight as the remainder had meandered up the river. Swein knew that Olaf hadn't seen them because he and his men had insisted on taking the lead. He was realistic enough to know that his actions might cause insurmountable problems in the future, but for now, he wasn't concerned.

The day passed quickly, in a blur of heightened awareness of every animal that watched their passage down the river. When they finally rowed into view of London in the late afternoon, Swein was amazed by the appearance of the town. It seemed to be only concerned with trade and not defence. He could see where a huge wooden bridge spanned the expanse of the river, still under construction, but it didn't stop the ships or boats that scurried busily underneath it. It was there to allow people to gain access to both sides of the land, London on the one and a smaller settlement on the other. He assumed it would have a name but he didn't know what it was.

Across the wooden expanse, he could see animals making a slow way, and people watching their approach with mild interest and then increasing alarm. It wouldn't be long until everyone knew that London was under attack.

If this town had been his to reinforce, as he almost wished it were, he'd have ensured it was closed off and well defended. He'd not have allowed enemy ships to beach near the walls of the dock, but that's exactly what was happening. Or what had been happening until he heard a cry of dismay from someone filled the air and the arrival of the hostile fleet was finally noted.

He watched with interest as those ships waiting to be unloaded or reloaded with whatever their cargo was, were quickly brought back into the full flow of the river, their intent to protect London clear. He would have ordered the same countermeasures as well. He grudgingly accorded the English some little respect for their belated activities.

From what Olaf had said to him he'd not expected such decisive movements from the men and women who lived in the town.

Olaf was busy issuing instructions, but Swein took the time to examine the site that Olaf had brought him to. It looked easier to conquer than the fortress on the hillside that he'd first shown him, Bamburgh, a place Olaf had already attacked. Yet London was clearly far bigger, and while the walls might not be in the best of repair, they were constructed of stone, and he suspected a deep ditch ran around the outer side of the wall as well.

Contrary to Olaf's words, London did not appear as though it would be easy to conquer, not at all. The men and women on the dock were working quickly, and with an ease and confidence that Swein suspected came from long practice, to ensure the waterway was blocked.

No matter how quickly Olaf organised his men to ram the rapidly growing structure of ships roped together and strung across the wide river, Swein knew he'd never make it in time. Effectively it looked as though the battle for London was over before it had even begun. But he doubted that Olaf would see it that way.

Along the stone walls of the city, he could see faces peeking out to look at the commotion on the waterfront. He was almost tempted to wave in welcome, the bright summery day lending a strange jovial atmosphere to their presence on the river but he refrained. They'd come as attackers, not as friends.

His men watched the activity, as did he, their oars resting on their legs where they were either raised high out of the water or serving as markers to stop the flow of the river sending them back out towards the sea they'd recently navigated. The men muttered softly to each other, but no one made any great effort to move. They were watching him and Olaf, and he wondered who they thought had the best idea.

Before them, Olaf had built his version of the growing ship bridge, and he had his men row so that they were closer to the

English vessels. Swein idly ordered some of his ships to reinforce Olaf's attacking fleet. It was clear that the attack wouldn't work but he needed to show support for his ally.

Ropes snaked between the ships to hold them close together, but the ships all strode with the strength of the river and Swein though it would be a brave man who chose to trust the moving floor beneath his feet and launch an attack. Swein thought it more likely that men would fall into the river and meet their watery end that way rather than in battle.

The flurry of activity spilling from the town wall and toward the dock alerted Swein that English warriors were coming. They brought with them the threat of sharpened metal and more alarmingly, a huge number of men and women prepared to fight for their livelihoods, armed with anything they could find that might dissuade the attackers.

At their front came a man holding an enormous golden cross and Swein smirked to see that in this Olaf hadn't lied. The English men genuinely felt that their holy men offered them protection against the raiders. He wondered how they'd feel when they discovered that the attackers were mostly as Christian as they were. It wouldn't be a battle about religion and gods, but one only about who could offer the best attack or defence. He already suspected that unless they did something drastic, the defence would be the victors. Olaf had been over confident when he'd chosen London as their focal point of attack. That was evident.

Swein considered a number of alternatives to the seemingly inevitable ship battle and dismissed them just as quickly. They could make landfall here and march on London, or they could make landfall and try and find horses and attack the surrounding countryside, or they could withdraw now and come again in the middle of the night, or they could just find an easier target. He knew that none of the options would appeal to Olaf, not now he'd come so far and made his intentions clear. Neither did Swein want his raid on England to descend into chaos and damage his reputation. That was not what this had been about.

Fire, he thought. Perhaps it would allow them to gain access to

London. It would be better than negotiating with the holy men stood on the wharf surrounded by warriors and their gleaming weapons, their shields slung over their backs and the great mass of men and women who were there as well, ready to defend if their warriors should inexplicably fall before the attackers. They were likely to be more deadly than the warriors because they fought with passion and resolve as opposed to the cold reasoning of men who fought for a living.

With fire, they could burn their way in, or at least burn the long wooden bridge and so try and cut off any aid that might come from the south. He had no idea how populated the land was around London. If they burnt the bridge and made it to shore, would its enemy surround London or would reinforcements come quickly from wherever the king and his jarls happened to be residing?

He thought about that. The king, as far as he knew, lived in the southern part of England, on the far side of the river. If they burnt the bridge that connected London with her king, then it would allow them time to gain a foothold in London and any reinforcements from the king himself would have to travel further to find another route. As Olaf had said, the Thames didn't cut England in two, but its source was far away and would make it difficult for any reinforcements to reach her unless they came from the land to the north of her.

Or by way of the river.

His thoughts were interrupted by the cries of wounded men, and he refocused on Olaf's temporary line of ships, surprised to find that they'd advanced close enough to attack the enemy. He'd expected Olaf to exercise more caution.

Instead, a minor battle was taking place as men balanced on the bobbing ships.

Olaf's warriors had made their way to the front of their ships where they pressed against the English fleet. They were forcing a path through the men assembled inside the hastily moved ships and were trying to steer the ships back towards the docks behind them. Swein watched carefully. He didn't want to be seen as being too slow to react to this unforeseen development, but neither did he want to commit his men if it looked unlikely to succeed. He still thought fire might be the only genuine alternative.

The air was filled with the angry shouts of the English people as they watched the first twelve men touch dry land and come racing towards them, weapons drawn. Olaf's warriors had come a long way for their treasure and it was unlikely that this token resistance by the people of London would dissuade them.

The holy man stepped bravely into the path of the first warriors; his hand raised before him and his followers sheltering behind him. For a moment Swein thought it might stop the fighters, but then a surge of activity at the wharf drew Swein's attention and he watched more of Olaf's men try to force their way over the hurdle of the English ships and onto the dock. Shields and swords, axes and seaxs glinted in the sunlight, a total contrast to the serene peace their arrival had disrupted.

The English hadn't given up yet though and had chosen fire as their last saviour, just as Swein had been considering it, and even as the warriors who'd made it to shore faced the bishop on the dock, the fire was being liberally spread along the ships they'd clambered over. There'd be no retreat for the men on dry land.

The smell of burning wood and pitch filled Swein's nostrils with their acrid stench as he watched Olaf to see what he'd do next. The exploits of the man grew with each retelling, but one fact was true. In none of his attacks did he ever leave his men to their death. No matter what odds befell him, he always rescued his men.

It gave Swein an idea.

He motioned his ship's captain to him, and the man quickly understood his instructions although his eyes opened wide with shock on hearing them. Swein nodded to show he meant what he was commanding, and the man touched each of the crewmen as he wound his way back towards the prow of his ship, telling them what they were to do.

Swein glanced one more time. It looked as though Olaf was going to leave his men after all. The fire was raging too brightly on the string of English ships pulled across the Thames for him to attempt any rescue mission and those of his warriors who could were rapidly returning to their own ships which were being cut loose from the inferno. But Swein had seen another way that the men could be reached and if Olaf didn't try it first, he would do it, and in that way win the thanks and the support of Olaf's supporters. It would be a sure way of enraging Olaf and doing it all in the name of keeping their force safe would only add to his anger.

He waited for a heartbeat, watching where the English warriors were surrounding the men, and then he waited for a further heartbeat, ensuring that Olaf was genuinely planning on leaving his men to their fate. Despite everything he'd ever heard about Olaf, it seemed clear that he wasn't going to order any of his ships to attack through the heat and muck of the fire. Not that it was an easy decision for Olaf. He and his men could be seen arguing angrily, some gesturing towards the fight and others gesturing back out towards the safety of the sea.

Swein indicated to his captain that he was to go ahead with his plans, and as one the men heaved on their oars and turned the ship so that it faced directly toward the dock. There was little fire because the English men and women hadn't wanted to burn the precious cargoes that sat on the dockside waiting to be loaded onto ships or transported into London itself. Guarding the goods was a handful of men, well equipped but with the air of those who didn't battle often and who perhaps were more skilled with practising warcraft than waging it.

His ship slipped quickly and silently toward the dock, and he pulled his axe free from its place on his weapons belt. To get to the men Olaf was abandoning he needed to step ashore, kill the guards and rush towards the small skirmish.

He was aided in his endeavour by the people of London who'd taken a giant step back from the battle and was slowly retreating through a gate behind them. He imagined that behind that gate the entire population of London waited for news that the raiders had been beaten or scared away.

The closer they came to the dockside, the more and more of

his shipmen stowed their oars inside the vessel and grabbed their weapons as well. He'd not be taking his first step onto English land alone.

The current was minimal as he watched the wooden pilings of the dock come closer and closer. With everyone's attention on the skirmish taking place not even the men on guard duty noticed the near silent approach.

He raised his finger to his lips to ensure all of his small force of twenty men remained silent and then he leapt onto the wooden dockside, reeling a little with the sudden change from the roll of the river to standing stationary. His ship harmlessly bounced against coiled ropes along the side of the dock, and he expected the guardsmen to shout in shock at the attack. But no cry came, and he was able to sneak up behind the first man, and without so much as a whisper of movement, his axe was at the man's throat and with a small slicing action the heat of blood covered him. His warriors similarly dispatched the other five guardsmen and then there was nothing more to be done but race towards the flaming ships and the men who were fighting for their lives on the far side of the dock.

He didn't even have time to see if Olaf or any of his men were watching his actions.

The day was warm, a gentle breeze on his face and as he ran he felt sweat slide down his face. Sparks from the fire were flying lazily through the air, and he swept one or two from his clothes before they had the opportunity to catch once more.

His path was relatively unobstructed. A man here, a women there, but he simply pushed them out of his way as he ran into the fray as though his life depended on it. The bishop and his cross were racing towards the gate but he let them go, his eyes narrowing as he caught the ice blue gaze of the man staring at him. He felt a moment of premonition but ignored it. No holy man would kill him. Not today. He prayed to the same God as fervently as the English did. He felt sure of it.

When he was within earshot, confident that his warriors were behind him, their reassuring weight moving the wooden beams of the dock beneath his feet, he shouted, his battle roar filling the air and obliterating all other sound.

The trapped men, so sure that this was their final battle, had formed a simple shield wall against the attacking English men. The English men stood between Swein and the warriors, and between the warriors and their chance to escape. Without pausing for thought, and although the English were slowly turning and raising an alarm that they were being attacked from behind as well as from in front, Swein swept into the English men. His axe was already bloodied. He leveled it at the turning head of a huge man with a dark brown beard and the build of a warrior from the old tales. The man fell before he could so much as whisper his anger and Swein turned his attention to the next man before he even heard the thud of the huge man hitting the wooden deck.

Behind him, Swein felt his warriors streaming past him into the gap he was forging. As his side split the English warriors, half to the side of him with Dryi performing the same blocking function on the other half of the split force, Swein roared for Olaf's men to rush through and find sanctuary on their ship.

The yells of the English men were thunderous, but Swein ignored them, instead listening to the ebb and flow of the battle and for the telltale sign that the last man had made good his escape. As he waited he fought against the raised shields of the English, taunting them with successive blows from his axe, daring them to react as aggressively as he was. But the intensity had drained from their attack and it took only moments longer for all the men who still lived to be rushing for his ship and for Dryi and him to be following them, their shields before them and their axes ready for any stray attack.

Swein kept waiting for the sound of a whistling arrow to reach his ears but nothing came and by the time he'd returned to his vessel, three more of his ships were there offering support.

Olaf's men clambered on board one of the ships and then they were rowing quickly back out to join the main force, the smell of the smoking ships hanging in the air and the smoke making their eyes water and tear.

Swein collapsed into the hull of his ship, a grin of delight on his face.

That would give his men something to talk about. They might not have won a victory here today, or not yet at least, but Swein had shown he was committed to the cause and that he would protect any of the men on the raid, no matter whether they looked to Olaf or himself.

He could well imagine that Olaf would be cursing him right now for his bravery. He certainly hoped he was.

Through his laboured breathing, he ordered his ship to be taken alongside Olaf's own and once there he grinned at the warrior, his good cheer for once matching Olaf's own and was rewarded with a broad smile of surprise from Olaf.

"I think London may be a little more problematic than I at first thought," Olaf said by way of an apology as Swein staggered to his feet, the after effects of his brief skirmish making his limbs heavy.

"I think you might be right. But there are still ways," he offered. While Olaf had been attacking, he'd been looking at London, assessing her for weaknesses. He'd found one at the dock, and he intended to find more. "The bridge will be our next attacking point," he said, nodding towards the large structure in the distance, without making his intention too clear.

The people of London had almost all retreated behind their walls and from the strong stone ramparts and occasional wooden repairs, they watched the vast fleet before them with worry and concern. Swein had won a small battle, nothing more. London had more to give and far, far more to be taken from it yet.

"The bridge?" Olaf said with surprise. "Why?"

"It'll cut London off from the king in the south, or so I understand it. If we take the bridge and attack quickly, no later than dawn tomorrow, the king will have no time to send reinforcements, and I think London has already revealed her strength in warriors and holy men as well," he added as an afterthought. Olaf was watching him carefully. He hadn't thanked Swein for saving his men, but Swein didn't think Olaf was the sort of person who would do so. As such his next words were a surprise.

"My thanks for saving my men," Olaf said quietly, all bluff gone from his voice. "I hadn't appreciated the danger I placed them in. And you my Lord Swein, well, I've heard tales of your greatness in battle but until now I've only ever half believed the voices of the skalds. It appears I was wrong to doubt you."

Olaf reached over the edge of his ship then with his huge arm, covered with shining metal rings, and he clasped Swein's hand firmly.

"We'll make good allies," Olaf said simply before turning away.

"And now to make a fire of their fledgeling bridge," Olaf said, as he signaled for his men to return to their ships. "We'll retreat a little way, let them think we're gone, and then we'll return with the daylight and our fiery morning."

Swein liked the sound of that and indicated that his men should follow suit. He'd entered the mouth of the Thames with no little trepidation, but he felt calmer now, more secure in himself. If even the great Olaf could thank him and appreciate his bravery, he felt sure his men would. All he needed was a great victory over the English, and he'd have the reputation he'd so long craved.

CHAPTER 6
London
AD994

S wein set a night watch that evening. Each ship had at least
one man, if not more, alert throughout the short summer's
night. They ate within their ships, and the men spoke softly
within their craft. The enemy knew they were there, but they did
nothing but watch them back. No one attempted to engage with
them, and Swein knew that come the morning the English would
be no better armed or able to put up any different sort of resistance.

He and Olaf spoke long into the light night, Swein worried that
just like in the far northern lands, the sun might never bleach
from the sky but remain all night long. When darkness finally
shielded them, he and his men began the work they needed to set
the wooden bridge ablaze. Each vessel was ordered to find some
spare wood, something dry and which they could survive without so that they could use it to set a fire burning in the hull of one
of the English crafts that they were going to steal away during the
night.

Most of the rest of the fleet would follow in its wake and would
then spill from their ships and alight on the London side of the
bridge, the northern side, but only when they knew no reinforcements would be coming from the king.

Then Swein would strike. He and three of his ships would attack the dock again, setting a fire close to the enclosing wall. Swein hoped that in the panic that ensued some of his men would manage to steal inside London itself and from there, well they could terrorise the inhabitants until they agreed to pay them a hefty weight in silver.

Swein hardly slept that night, buoyed by the success of his decision to rescue Olaf's men and the joy he felt sure was coming the next day when the rest of his plan came to fruition. He watched the stars all night long, wondering what they portended and was pleased when he decided it was light enough to launch the fire ship.

Olaf and the majority of the fleet set off behind the fire ship, not yet ablaze until they were closer to the wooden bridge, and Swein and his four ships made their way to the much closer dock.

He'd expected a guard to be set but in the pre-dawn light, the dock was deserted, the ships that hadn't been gutted by the fire were pulled up onto the wooden surface, and all the goods and supplies had been hastily removed. He glanced at where the gate was, again expecting to see some movement, but there was nothing, not even the flicker of a nightlight to make him think that the men and women of London feared another attack.

They were foolish, or they were so convinced another attack was coming they'd locked themselves up tight to guard against it. They must have hopes that stone walls, a deep ditch and the wooden ramparts that shored up some of the tumbled down wall, would do the work the warriors and bishop had failed to do the day before; deter the warriors and force them to reconsider their decision to attack.

Swein realised that the token resistance from the people of London had given him the resolve to attack London that he'd not yet felt. When Olaf had spoken of London, he'd made it appear as though it was a place filled with precious gems and piles of heavy silver, ripe for the taking, with men and women inside her who didn't know how to defend themselves. The truth was starkly different and far more appealing. Swein relished the challenge that London now presented. It was more attractive to take something from people when they valued it as much as he did.

He wanted to get inside the stone walls no matter what.

His men moved quietly as they brought their ships to the dock, spilling about two-thirds of the occupants of each ship onto the wooden planks and the rest pulling away just as quickly. Swein would not risk losing any of his men if the attack failed. Each commander was tasked with ensuring all of his men lived through the scuffle. Only when London was secure would Swein allow all of his men to disembark.

Dryi was his constant companion as they stepped as quietly as they could across the dock they'd raced across the day before and towards the stonewalls. His ears strained for any noise that showed they'd been discovered, but he heard nothing apart from the bleat of the goats inside the walls.

As Swein moved, he kept looking behind him, searching for the signs that the bridge was on fire until Dryi told him to keep his eyes forward in annoyance.

"They left at the same time as us. Give them the opportunity to at least reach the bridge before you start to worry."

Knowing that Dryi was correct, Swein focused on what he was supposed to be doing. It wasn't far to the stonewall and soon he and his men were sheltering beneath it, using the deep ditch, dry from the long summer, to shield themselves from view. They carried with them pieces of timber to start their fire, but Swein and Olaf had decided that the fire should only be started once the rest of the ships had reached the bridge. The people of London needed time to panic before the second fire was lit.

The wait seemed to go on forever, and every so often Swein had to hush the men from whatever conversation had sprung up amongst them. The men weren't fearful of any future altercation, in fact, if anything, they'd had to be reminded to bring shields as well as axes and their ships quantity of timber. Swein felt as though the attack had something of the feel of a celebration about it. That worried him slightly. He didn't think the attack would be easy, and he wanted his men to be battle ready if they needed to be, not lazily confident.

At his side, Dryi muttered softly so that stories of the Old Gods caught in the early morning chill air and drifted away towards the burgeoning daylight, but still no telltale signs of orange flames came from the mist shrouded view of where Swein knew the bridge was.

Swein began to worry and then he started to get annoyed with himself. Why had he let Olaf take the lead? He should have gone himself, ensured that everything went to plan.

"Patience, My Lord," Dryi said beside him, and Swein could happily have told Dryi to keep his peace, but Dryi was right. He knew patience. It was patience that had allowed him to assemble his father's allies against him and gain the kingdom for himself. Once more he thought what a pity it was that his father hadn't simply stayed away, that he'd been forced to kill him in the end.

Stray rumours had reached his ears throughout the long winter when he'd usurped his father's kingdom, of men who were living near to one of the part-completed trelleborg sites, who'd slaughtered enough of the inhabitants to allow them to live within its complexes. The news disturbed Swein but not as much as when he'd realised it was his father, trying to use his fortress to build followers and regain what he'd lost. Then the knowledge had calmed him as opposed to worry him.

It was good to know who his enemy was and to know that he and his father were both as well acquainted with the site in Skane as each other. Swein knew how to sneak inside just as much as his father knew how to sneak out.

With the better weather and the thawing of the snow Swein had wasted no time in mounting an attack against his father, one that had ended in his father's death at his hands, and the knowledge that his father had been even more delusional about his own powers than Swein had ever realised. When Swein had confronted his father, his clothing streaked with the blood of dead men; his father had still demanded his kingdom be returned to him, no matter the blood that ran without cease from his stomach wound, and the terrible stench of decay that had erupted from his injury.

His father had died swiftly on the end of Swein's sword. He could have left him to die from his infected wounds but at that moment he'd been weakened by love for a man who'd never cared for him, and he'd been unable to allow his father to suffer as much as he wanted him to. His father had actively worked to get his kingdom back, a country that no one wanted him to have but a few hundred men, and Swein had felt no remorse about killing the man. None at all.

If his father wouldn't accept the reversal of his fortunes, then he'd at least make sure his death was swift.

Dryi punched his arm and pulled him from his reverie. In the grey of the predawn, he could see orange flames beginning to make their way hungrily along the bridge. Swein smiled and his posture relaxed. Perhaps, after all, he was right to have sent Olaf to do the simple task of starting the fire. Now it was his turn to cause the most confusion.

Swein still waited, as did his men, watching the flames lick their way along the wooden structure, it so resembling tales of a dragon with a fiery breath from his youth that Swein suddenly saw the story brought to life before him.

Only when the fire was nearly half way along the part constructed bridge, and the first faint cries of panic were heard from behind the walls, did Swein call his men together and have them build their wooden structure before the gate into the town.

What had felt like huge pieces of wood as they'd carried them across the open expanse between their ships and the wall, materialised into a small collection of broken shields, oars and discarded rope and made only a small pile of fuel to burn. Still, it would have to suffice as they had no way of gathering more wood.

Swein ordered the fire to be set, and he and his men again sought shelter under the safety of the walls. They were all transfixed by the view of the bridge burning and yet although there had been some activity in London, Swein suddenly worried that the people of London wouldn't be tricked by their attempts to set fire to the whole place.

Swein supposed that behind their stonewalls the buildings

would be made of wood and turf and so easy to burn. But first they needed to get inside London, and as no one was in any great rush to get out, he realised that the people were probably seeking shelter inside knowing full well that while the bridge might burn down, and the gate might burn too, they were still safe inside.

He turned to Dryi then, a quirked smile on his face. It appeared as though they'd have to take even greater risks to capture London.

He beckoned his men to him and hastily gave instructions on what he wanted them to do. He, Dryi, Molti and Pallig, his future brother by marriage, had considered what they'd do if their ploy didn't work. Swein hadn't shared his worries with Olaf. Olaf didn't seem to understand the meaning of the word failure.

Dryi nodded to show he understood what he needed to do and set off to return to the dockside. He needed to call the ships back, get more men on the ground and have them disperse around the stonewalls of London. Once there, the plan was to set more and more fires, using whatever fuel they could find, and making it appear as though a far superior force surrounded the people of London than really did.

Pallig set off in one direction and Swein in the other. More men would catch them up.

As the sun began to peak over the horizon with welcoming pinks and reds, Swein turned his attention to the stonewall leading away from the dock. He and Dryi had purposefully chosen to head towards the back of the town. He secretly hoped that once more he'd be able to win greater renown for himself, but he was also realistic enough to know that he might be denied any further chances. They seemed destined to fail in their attempts to capture London and if he knew that then he was certain his men were only too aware as well.

Still, there was the smallest possibility that some way through the walls could be found and he was prepared to take try once more.

A loud tolling noise was coming from within the walls, a church bell warning everyone that London was under attack and

Swein hoped it meant that everyone was running to the source of the fire, at the new bridge, and not to guard the other gates.

It was a slim hope, and he knew it. Dryi caught up with him quickly as he skirted his way through the deep ditch. He wasn't sure what he was hoping to find as he rushed along the wall and ditch but he knew he'd see it when he saw it, an opportunity, or a possibility too good to miss, some weakness, some overlooked repair work, anything that might allow them inside.

From the other side of the wall, he could hear the worried shouts and calls of the people within. Dogs barked, goats bleated and so too did frightened women and children. He almost pitied them. They'd thought themselves safe within the thick walls, and he and Olaf had come to prove that wasn't the case. Not at all.

Or so he hoped.

Swein was starting to think that the walls of London were just as well constructed as he'd been lead to believe, impassible unless someone inside could open the gates and allow them admission and that wasn't going to happen. Perhaps they should have sent a small force masquerading as traders to gain admittance. Then, when the inhabitants slept, they could have opened the gates and allowed their comrades inside. It was an intriguing idea but one for another day. Yesterday they'd made mistakes, and they needed to try and right those errors.

In front of him, Swein finally noticed something that might prove useful. A tumble of ancient stonework lay across the deep ditch, its white stone aged and crisscrossed with green plants that hadn't let the stonework stand in their way when they grew. It was firmly anchored to the ground by the reaching arms of weeds and trees both.

The section almost filled the ditch, and Swein rushed to it, hardly daring to breathe in his excitement. Was this what he'd been looking for?

Swein tested the stability of the stonework by kicking it with his foot, and confident that it would hold, he clambered over the stones, weeds and thistles trying to hamper his work. He was pleased he'd worn his leather gloves. The stone pieces were huge, and he had to reach with his clawed fingers to find any purchase, but eventually he managed to reach the top of the rocks and take in the view before him.

The stones filled the ditch to about the height of a man, but as he peered into the lightening day, he could see no corresponding space in the thick wall. The stones might have tumbled from this spot, but it had been so long ago that the replacements were only an assortment of smaller stones with added wooden ramparts. Swein sighed in disappointment. This would not allow them inside London. It was a weakness in the wall but one that the inhabitants of London had laboured to make whole again.

"Is it an opening?" Dryi called to him from his place within the ditch. No one else had followed Swein up the fallen stone, and twenty men now looked at him with curious eyes.

"No, the wall's been repaired. We'll have to keep looking."

Dryi shrugged in acceptance, his fingers itching to reach out and claim one of his arrows and fire it at the enemy if they appeared while his king was unprotected. The rest of Swein's men began to make their way out of the ditch so that they could skirt the obstruction. Swein turned his back for a brief moment, trying to catch a glimpse of the fire near the bridge, and at that moment an arrow shot over the wall and clattered onto the stone surface beneath his feet.

Swein looked about in shock. The arrow had missed him, but only by about a foot.

Another arrow followed it as Swein rushed to the end of tumbled down stonewall and jumped clear of it, and the ditch both. Dryi had his hand on his bow and was aiming an arrow back over the thick wall of London as the rest of the men rushed to form a shield wall to protect their king.

Swein landed in an untidy heap of legs and arms, the height he'd jumped from knocking the breath from his lungs. He was grateful for the quick reactions of his men and Dryi and even more pleased when he heard larger projectiles impact the hastily constructed shield wall.

"Dryi, to me, now," Swein called. He wanted to retreat, but he wouldn't do so without his archer.

When Dryi didn't return as quickly as he thought he should have, Swein stood and with his shield in front of him looked to where he knew Dryi had been standing.

Dryi was huddled against the fallen stonework, his shield above his head as he tried to protect himself from a heavy onslaught of rocks, spears and arrows from their faceless enemies.

Dryi was well and truly trapped.

"Men, we need to rescue Dryi. We'll move as one. Ensure everyone's head and back are protected."

His twenty men shuffled closer together as they made ready to retrieve Dryi, obeying his orders instinctively. Swein waited a moment or two, just waiting to see if the English ran out of missiles. When that seemed unlikely, he gave the command to walk forward.

Five men stood at the front of their strange moving shield wall, Swein now one of them, and five behind them while a further five covered the rear and the other five held their shield high enough to cover the rest of the men.

Swein wanted to get close enough to Dryi that he could retreat to the safety of everyone else's shields. It was difficult going, though. The ditch was steep and the men had to work hard to keep their footing and hold their position.

The English inside London, still unseen, had realised what they were doing and had started to pummel the shields of the rescuers. Anything and everything was being thrown at them from old pots to heavy pieces of stone. Swein felt each and every impact as they reverberated along the shields and into his arms. He gritted his teeth against the sensation.

Swein was pleased when he felt Dryi squeeze between his legs and find his shelter.

"Apologies, My Lord," Dryi gasped, but Swein clasped him on the back of his head in pleasure, and ordered the men to retreat along the ditch so that they could move far enough away from the wall that they were out of range.

Working their way back up the ditch was even more challenging than walking back into it. Eventually, and with the derisive shouts of the English ringing in their ears, the small collection of men managed to reach flat land and worked their way far enough away from the wall that not even the archer could reach them.

Swein ordered the men to drop their shields when the wall of London was a distant sight on his eye line. They were all breathing heavily, and the majority of them had bloody scrapes on their faces.

"Apologies, My Lord," Dryi said once more but Swein brushed his words aside. It wasn't his fault.

"I think London might well have beaten us," he said, and the men all nodded tiredly in agreement.

"Come, we need to get back to our ships and sail away from here. Sod Olaf and his 'London will be easy' attitude. It isn't and it's not. We need to attack somewhere else."

The men tiredly staggered to their feet and began the walk back towards the river. They'd walked along way in the predawn light and accomplished nothing. The Thames was a haze before them, and although Swein squinted into the distance, he could see no sign of fire raging from anywhere.

The attack had been an unmitigated disaster.

They slipped away from London under cover of night. Those who'd had the misfortune to be wounded in the unsuccessful attacks grumbled about their injuries while those who hadn't been injured made good on their lack and rowed that little bit harder.

England was proving to be less than the friendly place Olaf had assured them it was.

Dryi was slightly wounded with cuts and grazes where an arrow had glanced off his shoulder, but other than that was simply too apologetic about his lack. Swein had heard enough of his apologies and had rather peremptorily sent him to watch events on Pallig's ship rather than listen to him anymore.

Swein was angry and annoyed in equal measure. All of his men that he'd sent to find an entranceway into London had failed in their attempts, and he knew it hadn't been their fault. He should have been far stronger with Olaf, told him that they needed to start with a target where they could guarantee a win. Swein wasn't troubled by either failure or hard work, but putting his men and his ships in such harm's way, deliberately, grated on him.

He'd put too much trust in Olaf, the first and only time during his reign he'd trusted anyone other than his brother, his sister or Dryi, and he'd been a fool to do so. He should have found out more information for himself rather than trusting his men, and the wealth of his country, on a raid that seemed doomed to failure as soon as he'd seen the almost completed wooden bridge and the massive stonewalls that surrounded London and the smaller ones that encircled the docks.

Olaf had made it clear he wished to speak to him, signaling for him from his ship, but Swein had pretended he'd not seen his entreaties and had forced his men to row as quickly as they could so that he could get away from him.

He wanted to be on the open sea before he did anything else and assured that he and his men wouldn't be attacked by the English for their impetuous attack.

If the ships he'd left at the mouth of the Thames were surprised by his sudden reappearance the ships captains and the rest of the men didn't show it. Instead, they reported that there'd been no movement either in or out of the Thames since they'd disappeared from view and it was when Swein was talking with the captains that Olaf finally caught up with him. He brought his ship in close to Swein's own and Swein could see immediately that even his good cheer had disappeared.

Olaf's face was hooded in shadow and the light from the lamp burning in each of the three ships.

"Damn the bloody English," he began, Olaf's disappointment clear to hear. "The men who told me of London told me of their great stonewalls but failed to inform me that they stood as high as three or four men in places and were too thick to breach. They also neglected to mention their fierce resolve."

Swein had decided that he needed to try and salvage something from their alliance, and he listened to Olaf's excuses for some time, long enough to realise that he was genuinely disappointed. Perhaps, after all, men who'd known no better had led them both on a fruitless journey.

"We should raid inland," Olaf said when he'd finally stopped complaining. "The inhabitants of England will be on guard against another attack, but we have time yet to take them unprepared. I doubt word has even reached the king of the closeness of the raid."

"Where do you suggest we invade?" Swein asked, working hard to keep the anger and resentment from his voice at finally hearing Olaf say what he'd been thinking since the beginning of their partnership.

"To the south still. We should sail south, and as soon as we see a settlement of reasonable size, we should take it, and then raid further inland, leaving half of our men to guard the ships and allowing the other half to try their luck against the English."

Swein considered the idea. It was true that he couldn't just return to Denmark, not yet, he needed to gain something from the trip, or his kingship would suffer, but Olaf's good luck seemed to have run out and Swein was no longer sure he wanted to be in an alliance with the man."

He thought quickly, aware his men and Olaf's own were listening to their conversation.

"I agree. We should travel south for another two days at most and find somewhere else to attack. The English King's Winchester, it's not on the coast is it?"

He asked the question out of idle curiosity and the desire to irritate, amused by the transient expression of disbelief that flew over Olaf's face.

"No, it's inland," Olaf answered curtly, and Swein felt a grin trying to tug at his wind-weathered face. Sometimes it seemed as though even Olaf lost his good humour when he was confronting someone prepared to be even more daring in their actions.

"Then we need another place of importance to head towards. Do you have any suggestions?"

"No. But I've never been south from here, only ever north,

Maldon was north of here and so was Bamburgh. Well, you know where Bamburgh is, I showed you on the way here. We should head south."

Swein inclined his head in agreement. He was keen to explore more of the lands of the English. He had a desire to see Winchester, no matter that Olaf implied it was impossible.

"Although, we could try and reach Canterbury. It's one of the holiest places and near to the coast, or so I here."

Swein considered that for barely a heartbeat.

"No, we need to go somewhere that's not filled with people, that's not as large as London."

Swein managed to keep the censure from his voice when he mentioned London. He'd decided to give Olaf a second chance and making snide comments would only cause difficulties between them.

"We should keep the majority of the force at sea and send some of the ships to scout. Then, when they've found a suitable place for the rest of the fleet, we can call them in and make our camp."

"I agree," Pallig said at Swein's side, but Olaf was quiet while he considered the options.

"Fine, it's a good plan. We'll go further south, for no more than two days. Ten of the ships will skirt close to the shore, five of my ships and five of yours. You and I will be amongst the men," Olaf said, indicating Swein as he spoke, "while Pallig and my commanders maintain order amongst the rest of the fleet."

That was the problem with splitting the fleet. He did trust Pallig, he supposed, but still, he'd be happier if he were in two places at once. It had been his suggestion to have some of the fleet scout the land, and it would be churlish to argue over the details now.

"Agreed. We'll stay together tonight and then tomorrow we'll separate."

Olaf looked about as happy about the arrangement as Swein felt, but at least they'd reached an agreement, and their alliance hadn't disintegrated with their failure. It would be easy to take his fleet home, but with nothing to show for the effort and expense he'd incurred, and the loss of his reputation, he was happy to stay. For now.

The night passed too quickly, and bleary-eyed, Swein and the other four ships he'd chosen rowed closer to the shore to meet with Olaf and his five ships, while every other vessel was rowed out to sea, the wind having died with the sunrise.

There was some grumbling from the men, but overall, they were happy that they'd be given a second chance to attack the English. Their failure from the day before hadn't dented their enthusiasm for the task at all.

Olaf's good spirits had been restored as he shouted a cheery greeting to Swein and indicated the coastline they sailed within sight of. They stayed far enough away from the coast that they couldn't make out all the details of people and homes. They could see the curve of the cliffs and the beaches, the coves and the bays, and Swein's belief that they'd find somewhere suitable to moor the ships grew the further they travelled.

The land was open and inviting, much like his own and in stark contrast to the fjords of the kingdom Olaf claimed.

For an entire day they journeyed along the coast and spent another night on the sea but the following day, they came across a wide expanse of sandy shore, too good an opportunity to miss. Swein signaled to Olaf at the same time that Olaf indicated to Swein, and together the ten ships crept closer and closer to the shore. Olaf indicated that he would go ashore and Swein let him go without any misgivings. The sand looked inviting, and he could determine no sign of any dwellings along the grassy cliffs. It looked as though they'd found somewhere that was almost deserted.

It would be the perfect place for the men to shelter and rest after their failure in London. Swein let Olaf lead the way, but as soon as Olaf and his men had disembarked from his ship, Swein indicated that he wanted to ground his ship on the sandy bank. He wanted to set foot in England for the first time and without Olaf's smirking grin watching his every move.

His ship came to rest on the shore, and he jumped into the surf and strode onto the soft sand. The sea was retreating around him as his men accompanied him up the slight incline. In the distance, he could see Olaf's men scrambling up the grassy banks to higher ground. He let them go and indicated that some of his men should take a watch while he walked along the beach.

It felt good to feel the ground almost solid beneath his feet after so long at sea but he realised that the tide had a lot further to go as it swirled past his ship. He'd need to move it in case they needed to make a quick escape.

His ship's captain had stayed within his vessel, and he ran down the beach towards him. He wanted to instruct him before it was too late. But his captain was already more than aware of the imminent danger as Olaf's ship was very close to being stranded by the retreating tide. Swein raced past Olaf's ship shaking his head at his foolishness. He and his men helped push his ship back into the swirling flow, but he didn't climb on board. He wanted to stay longer. See what Olaf discovered.

Swein hoped this would be a good place to bring the rest of his ships to. As he turned to see where Olaf was, he was surprised to see him and his men running back towards the ship. Was there an enemy after all?

He shouted to Olaf, but he shook his head, his concern only with his ship. Swein watched in surprise as his men grabbed hold of the stricken Long Serpent and picked her up to ensure she stayed in the water. When their work was done, Olaf returned to Swein, his breath a little ragged but his usual grin back on his face.

"This'll be a good place. We should call the men here. There are a few houses in the distance, and I can see smoke from fires. If we raid inland, we'll find the English, and we'll be able to attack."

Swein searched Olaf's face for any sign of dishonesty, but the man was speaking the truth. He needed a victory as much as Swein did.

"Very well. Call the ships in, and we'll spend the night on the beach. Come the morning we'll march out with half of the forces and find somewhere to attack."

"You are too cautious Swein," Olaf said to him jovially, although a hint of menace hung in the air, the censure evident for all that he was trying to make light of his beliefs. "You need to be brash in your actions. Take some risks. If you don't take any chances, then the Gods can't offer you their support."

Swein grimaced to hear Olaf speak so openly of his perceived faults.

"Kings have more to think about than treasure," Swein responded, his anger not showing but he knew it bubbled beneath the surface. Olaf was trying to undermine his belief in himself.

"I wouldn't know, King Swein," Olaf replied darkly, his intent clear. He wanted to be a king, and he planned on being one, and soon at that.

"When you and I are both kings we should return to this conversation," Swein rejoined, his temper flaring just a little. He stalked away from Olaf. He didn't want to say anything he might regret. Not now that they'd agreed to attack the English from the beach.

Swein's men were pleased to both be on dry land and also to know that they'd soon have an opportunity to do more than watch an unsuccessful attack on London. Swein shared their pleasure. He wanted to accomplish something more during this attack on England.

With the sunrise, half of his men began the work of making some temporary defensive structures to protect the beach whereas the rest set off to discover the habitations they could attack and steal their wealth from.

Swein felt the spirit of the assault infuse him. The land was rich and fertile, bursting with sheep and well-tended fields and he didn't doubt that the people who lived there would be prosperous.

CHAPTER 7

Near Margate
September AD994

S wein rubbed his bloody hand across his face. Once more he and his men had been involved in a minor clash. It was never a full force of the English that came against them, but it was always enough for his men to feel deflated. They'd been on English land for nearly two weeks now and to date they'd found nothing of great value apart from horses that they'd used to expand their search base.

Swein couldn't deny that he was disappointed and frustrated by the failure of his fleet in England. His men were unhappy and grumbling and he couldn't even berate them. Especially not when Olaf and his men remained so unfailing cheerful about the whole thing.

Every night Olaf promised that the next day they'd find great treasure, and every day Swein hoped and his hopes came to nothing.

If England was as rich and prosperous as Olaf believed it to be, the people on this strip of land were doing a remarkably good job of hiding it from the raiders.

The people they'd come across today, no more than a scouting party for some larger force, had shown no fear in attacking Swein and his group of thirty men, none at all, and now they were dead or injured but they'd succeeded in stopping Swein advancing any further that day.

Five of his men had deep gashes along their legs and arms, and they would have to retreat back to their ships.

"My Lord," Dryi called softly, bringing his horse in line with Swein's own. "I don't like to talk of defeat but we should leave now. The men and women are more interested in their harvest than they are in making a war against us, and the English King hasn't even sent a representative to treat for a peace. There's nothing here for us, no matter what Olaf promises."

Dryi had been saying the same thing for the best part of a week and his words were starting to wear down Swein's resolve because they seemed to be so truthful. He'd expected a battle along the lines of Olaf's attack at Maldon. He'd not expected the English king to completely ignore them.

Instead of his normal annoyed response, he agreed with his friend.

"You're right Dryi. There's nothing for us here. We need to go somewhere else, seek an enemy we can actually attack, not one who ignores our presence and leaves their farmers to counter us."

Dryi, his own face streaked with blood and mud, looked surprised to hear Swein agree with him.

"What of Olaf?" he asked, and Swein shrugged.

"What of him? He can stay or go as he pleases. I'll bring a formal end to our alliance and then I think we should continue our journey around the bottom of England, make our way to the Dublin Norse."

"Don't you think we should just head for home? You were worried that there might be treachery in your absence. If we return now no one will have had time to move against you."

"And that's the problem," Swein responded acerbically. "We need to allow whoever the enemy is time to make themselves known. If I don't, I might never know who works against me."

Dryi considered the wisdom of that as the rest of the men searched the bodies of the dead men, removing anything of value from them. This might well be the only trinket they had to show for their great voyage to England.

"I disagree, My Lord," Dryi said and Swein smirked at him.

"I didn't expect us to agree on two different things in the same day. Come, we'll return to the men, get them started on our retreat from England."

For just a moment longer, they both stared at the landscape before them. It had promised so much but now they knew it was almost denuded of inhabitants and there was little portable wealth to be found.

"We'll come again," Swein muttered to himself and beside him Dryi turned sharply to stare at him.

"My Lord?" he queried but Swein turned his horse and headed back to the coast.

"We'll come again, with better intelligence and without Olaf. I fear his presence has poisoned every decision I've made."

The men took the news well, Olaf didn't.

"My Lord Swein," he muttered, his anger breaking through his good humour for only the second time in Swein's experience. "It's too soon to break off the attack. The English always take time to warm up to an invasion."

"My Lord Olaf," Swein responded, stressing the 'Lord' although Olaf was lord of nowhere yet. "It's been near enough three weeks, and I've five coins to show for my trouble and some of my men have nothing but festering wounds and the promise of a painful death."

Olaf paced around Swein's tent with annoyance.

"We've had some bad luck, but the English will come," Olaf repeated said, but Swein had heard enough.

"The English might have filled your treasure chests with silver three years ago but I don't think they're at all concerned by your return, or by my being here. They send only a handful of men against us but they do enough to dissuade us from further attack and Olaf, it's worked."

"I've no desire to kill simple farmers trying to harvest their crops. Their wealth is all in the ground and I don't plan on harvesting it for them. My men and I need treasure, not crops, something to take home with us, not horses that can't be transported because we don't have enough room in the ships. We're leaving. You can stay, I've no problem with that, although I think it's pointless."

"Without you the force will only be a third as strong as it should be."

"It doesn't matter whether it's at full strength or not. The English aren't coming to meet us in battle and if they don't come then their king won't treat with us and offer us money to leave. We don't have an enemy at the moment Olaf, can't you see that?"

Olaf's face was angry, his eyes a stormy blue, but Swein knew he was doing the right thing.

"I want us to part as allies, not enemies," Swein said, hoping the words sounded truthful. He and Olaf might have had no success but the possibility of their joint raid had kept them as almost allies for over eight years now. He didn't want to undo all the goodwill.

"We'll part as allies, Swein," Olaf responded, "but I can't hide my disappointment, and my men will know it for what it is and they'll talk about it and the other jarls of our own countries will hear of it."

"That's no threat for me, Olaf," Swein responded. "The season is too late, the men concerned only with the harvest and my own men wish to be home before the winter storms."

Olaf watched him speculatively and Swein assumed he knew he was lying to him. Whether Olaf chose to question him more closely was something that would make itself plain in the next few moments and Swein knew the perfect way to test him.

"Now tell me. Who moves against my kingdom?"

"No one – not yet," Olaf responded as he gazed at the great expanse of men making ready to leave England. Already twenty of the ships were out at sea, their colourful sails in the process of being raised for the journey.

"The wind blows in the wrong direction for sails," Olaf muttered absent-mindedly but Swein chose to ignore him.

"Then when?" Swein pressed, trying to take advantage of Olaf's distraction but Olaf didn't respond.

"At least tell me who?" Swein pressed but Olaf seemed ignorant of his questions, just as he'd ignored Olaf's question to him about the sails. Resolutely Olaf faced him, his hand held to offer him an arm clasp of friendship. It appeared as though he was going to forget that Swein was blatantly lying to him about the destination of the fleet.

"You have many enemies Swein," Olaf spoke quietly so that Swein had to strain to hear him over the noise of the men. "Many enemies Swein. Let's hope I'm not added to those who mean you ill will."

And with that Olaf was gone, sweeping along the dunes to where his own men still camped. Swein watched him go with some relief. Everything he did seemed to pale into insignificance when Olaf was near. Even with his antics in London, rescuing Olaf's men, it was still Olaf that men watched with intrigued eyes, and Olaf that they hoped to emulate. It would be far easier when he was no longer a part of their endeavor.

CHAPTER 8
The Shetlands
AD995

He'd cautioned his men to silence, and yet on the still night they seemed almost incapable of following his instructions. Swein could have let his anger and rage have their way with him, but no, if he was to have any semblance of silence, he needed to lead by example. If Swein gave vent to his true feelings he knew that the men would first erupt in a bubble of noise and only then actually listen to his words.

What he was asking them to do wasn't the most pleasant of tasks, but they had all agreed that they would need to seek vengeance on Olaf. He'd played them all for stupid men and now they needed to exact some revenge.

It was unfortunate for Olaf that they'd managed to track him down here, at Sigurd's hall on Mainland Shetland as he attempted to make his way towards his destination – to claim the kingdom of Norway. Unfortunate for Olaf, but fortunate for him. He'd been making his way back to his kingdom when he'd landed at Mainland Orkney and heard the unlooked for news that Olaf was slinking his way back to Norway with his ships filled with more and more treasure that the weak English king, Æthelred II had plied him with in order to have his fleet leave England's coast alone.

Swein had heard the news of Olaf's good fortune whilst he'd been raiding in Ireland. His rage had been immense and still it burned bright, far too bright. The fucking bastard Olaf had managed to exact so much treasure this time that he'd be far richer than Swein was, and Swein had a kingdom to tax and command.

Swein knew he should have kept a closer eye on Olaf and his devious ways, but it had looked as though their raid on England was doomed to failure. They'd done little but fail to take London, fail to even get inside the great stone walls of London, and then when they'd raided throughout Kent Swein had accomplished little but to give himself an injury by falling from his horse.

When Olaf had said he was staying behind, that he knew sooner or later the English would approach and offer them good silver to leave, Swein had thought him a fool and had left. Swein could still hear Olaf's derisory laughter as his fleet had sailed out to open sea.

Now that he knew how well Olaf had done, he had every intention of killing him, taking his wealth and using it to fund his own expeditions against England. If there were still riches to claim then he wanted to be the man to demand them and he'd learned valuable lessons from Olaf.

Swein needed to sit and wait, make a base for his men to raid from and then sooner or later the English would come, lead by their bishops and offer good treasure for his raiding force to leave. Next time, he vowed, he'd take fewer men but make their camp more permanent, build wooden walls and dig a ditch, show the English that he meant to make a stand and that he wasn't to be put off.

He'd not attack a sizeable target the next time, but ensure he positioned himself somewhere that would be menacing.

His fleet of ships, sixty in total, were making their way into the various harbours around Sigurd's hall as quietly as they could. Swein wanted them to attack Olaf and his thirty ships that were grounded on the beach closest to Sigurd's hall. His scouts had told him as much, and Swein wanted his own ships to be far away from them when they beached so that they could sneak up on them and kill them all while they slept.

For himself, Swein was going to make his way to Sigurd's hall, inside which Olaf and his men were feasting, and he was going to bar the door and set fire to the whole place.

He'd ensured a messenger went to Sigurd with details of his plans, but as he'd been unable to give a precise time for his attack, Swein could only hope that Sigurd survived what was about to happen.

Provided that Olaf was dead at the end of the night, Swein would be happy. He hoped he wouldn't kill Sigurd but he was proving to be difficult to manage and Swein hadn't categorically decided to keep the man alive. Not yet.

If he could kill all of Olaf's men as well, or turn them to his own cause, that would be an added bonus.

It was a pity for Olaf that Bjorn the trader had landed in Orkney only two days ago, and then gone straight to Birsay with the news of Sigurd's unexpected guests. It was even more unfortunate that Bjorn had told the news to Swein. Swein grinned at the delightful turn of events. It was auspicious for him.

Swein allowed his ship to beach itself on the far side of Mainland Shetland. He'd decided that he and his men would make their way across the small strip of land there and come to Sigurd's mighty hall from the east. It would confuse those within the hall if they tried to retaliate, and it would give him and his men the knowledge that provided they ran fast enough, the enemy wouldn't know where their ship was and wouldn't try and fire it.

Any who escaped from the hall would expect them to be on the west and they'd waste precious time searching for them there first. If any of them lived through the inferno and the deadly attack on the sleeping ship men, that was.

Swein would have to compensate Sigurd for the destruction of his hall, but then, he needed to gain the upper hand with Sigurd. He was growing in power and stature, and like Olaf, was beginning to think he owed nothing to the King of Denmark.

It was full dark by the time his ship's commander had beached the ship where Swein wanted it. The man had done little but bitch and moan since Swein had commanded him to come to Shetland. He'd said it was the wrong time of year, that a storm was brewing and that they needed to concentrate on getting home to

Aggersborg, but Swein had ignored him.

Swein respected the man but he wasn't about to let him dictate policy to his king.

Olaf needed to die and this was the perfect opportunity to do it with as little risk to his own men as possible. The knowledge that Olaf had all of his thirty ships with him, and also a representative from the English King, had given him pause for thought. It seemed as though the numbers were so clearly in his favour that the attack would be easy to accomplish. Good fortune such as that didn't necessarily assure him victory though, and he felt a little wary. He hoped this wasn't a trick from the old Gods.

Into the quiet evening air, Swein and his men disembarked from their ship, splashing through the chill water briefly before their feet encountered dry land. They carried two firebrands with them lit from a small lamp on the ship so that they could use it to set the hall on fire, but other than that they were relying on the light from the moon, even as shadowed as it was with rapidly scudding clouds.

There was a hint of an approaching storm but Swein thought they had time yet. He hoped that the two firebrands would be unnoticed by the guards Sigurd would have set, or that they would pass from sight with a blink and be instantly forgotten about. He didn't want anyone to raise the alarm before he was well and truly in position.

Swein didn't want to lose Olaf when he had him locked down in one place.

Sigurd knew he was coming, provided the messenger had reached him, and that was all.

Olaf had a substantial force with him. Thirty ships in total, if they'd all survived their attacks on the English, and that didn't include those that the English jarl had brought with him.

Swein wasn't overly enamored of the English king. It wasn't that he was a weak man; it was that he didn't seem to give any impression of being any sort of man. He'd not ridden to relieve London when they'd attacked and his failure to mount any sort of resistance was an oversight that Swein couldn't comprehend.

They might have tried to fire the bridge that was still under construction but he knew that London could have been reinforced by ships sent along the Thames or by men from the northern side of the river. At the time he'd been pleased that no reinforcements had come, but he now thought it a sign of weakness.

That London had proven to be impossible to gain admittance to was a thing of little note, some show of force should still have been ordered by the English king before he began to count his silver weight and hand it to Olaf.

Swein's eyes were on the great hall of Sigurd's and the buildings that surrounded it, and he belatedly noticed that silence emanated from it. Momentarily Swein worried that the men and women inside the hall had been alerted to his presence and were even now hiding from him and his men, or had slipped away in their own ships. Swein had sailed around the far side of the island, sending half of his men to stave off any attempt at retreat and so he didn't know how many ships were beached. It was possible that some had escaped.

Still, Swein walked on, carefully placing each foot so that he didn't misstep in the dim light from the moon over the dune and the farmland. It was late and he should be seeking sleep not vengeance but it was retaliation that drove him onwards in the chill nighttime air.

Within ten steps of the hall, lying in shadow under the light of the dim moon, he stopped and listened, the sound of his own heartbeat ringing loudly in his ears as he strained to hear the tell-tale noise of a group of people inside the hall. Then he heard it, the sound of the skald's voice raised and lowered as he wove his tale of heroes and beasts. That would more than explain the silence from inside the hall. Swein knew the power of men who could weave stories and spellbind their audiences. It was a rare skill and one many trained to acquire and which some were lucky enough to born with.

For a long moment Swein paused, wavering between his attack on many innocent people who were simply offering hospitality to Olaf on his journey north and his need for revenge against the man whose every move seemed blessed by whichever God he elected to revere.

Ultimately Swein knew what he needed to do without even considering it. Olaf was too much of a threat to his kingdom and his dreams. He'd tried to ally with him and that had been a disaster. Swein needed to salvage what he could from their alliance.

Swein turned and made his way back to his group of men who'd waited some distance from the hall. He took the firebrand from the man who'd carried it for him and, ensuring his seax was clear of its scabbard, and his other weapons were in place around his belt, Swein stepped close to the side of the hall, so close he imagined he could hear the inhabitants inside breathing, and he thrust the brand into the turf roof of the hall above one of the doorways. At the same time, he indicated to his men that they should rush forward with the four oars they'd brought from the ship to bar the wooden door and stand ready. He didn't want the door shut just yet. He needed to send his men in to ensure that Olaf was inside and that he was murdered so that the fire could cover his actions.

On the other side of the hall, Dryi was mirroring his actions having run round to do so at Swein's command. Others raced forward to add lumps of dry sea grass and discarded animal dung to the smoldering fire, and the wind chose that moment to gust along the fledgling fire and spread it so that it crackled over the turf roof in a shower of sparks, catching light immediately in the dry grasses.

Quickly the fire took hold and Swein directed his men to rush inside the hall. He wanted to ensure as many of Olaf's men as possible died and he wasn't prepared to rely on the fire to do the job itself.

Swein stood in the now open doorway, his men blocking it from either side, and by the other entrance, Dryi and his men did the same with the other door.

The hall swiftly erupted in a howl of screams and bellows of fear. Swein felt a grin slide onto his face and he tugged as his beard, ensuring it was free from his clothing before he made his foray inside the building. A body rushed past him and with the glow of the fire behind them, he could tell that it was a woman and a small child.

"Let them pass," Swein bellowed and his men did so. He wouldn't be feeling quite so generous with everyone who tried to escape.

The next figure to erupt from the smoking hall was a man wearing a byrnie and a weapons belt. He dashed towards Swein, his eyes open in shock and horror, and Swein allowed himself the time to think about his next act.

Swein shrugged with indifference, waiting to see which way the man ran, and when he saw him racing to meet him, there was no other choice. As the man tried to slide past him, Swein struck with his seax and the weapon easily went through the man's padded tunic. Swein felt blood rush between his hands, and he laughed mockingly at the surprised expression on the man's face as he folded in on himself, gurgling bright red fluid in the dark night.

His first kill and it had all been too easy.

More and more people were trying to escape and Swein beckoned his men inwards. He wanted Olaf's men dead and preferably by the sword. He didn't want to risk anyone escaping.

Battle rage evident in the eyes of his followers, Swein watched with satisfaction as one man, and then two and then ten rushed inside the hall, some colliding with those trying to make good their escape and some falling to their knees when weapons impacted their body.

Many would die tonight, and Swein hoped that amongst their number Olaf and his most fearsome warriors would also fall. He particularly wanted to ensure Horic and Axe died. They were both capable of avenging Olaf's death if he died tonight and they somehow managed to escape.

Swein was relying on his other shipmen to kill as many of Olaf's allies as possible, those who slept on the beach and on the ships.

They'd been arrogant in their victory in England because Swein had encountered no guards around the hall. Either that or

Sigurd had purposefully called off any guards so that he wouldn't put their lives at risk as well. Swein thought the latter. Olaf was a cocky bastard most of the time and also liked his men to share in his success.

Swein imagined that as many as possible had been invited inside Sigurd's hall to hear the voice of the skald. Olaf was an expansive leader who was always happy to share his good fortune.

The fire had thoroughly caught hold of the room and he could hear coughing coming from inside the building, as well as high-pitched cries of terror. He allowed any women or children who raced outside to find clean air and to go unharmed. It was Olaf he wanted, not innocents.

Above the roar of the fire as it consumed the grass roof, Swein could hear the clash of weapons inside the hall. He hoped that meant they'd found Olaf. Unable to contain his impatience any further, Swein stepped to the doorway, the heat of the fire washing over him as great plumes of smoke rushed through the entrance way. To the other side of the double entrance way he could see the same thing happening.

He squinted through the smoky air, trying to find Olaf. He could see where the central fire had been disturbed and strewn across the hall, almost making escape from the far side of the hall impossible, but he could also see his men making their way over the seeking flames by climbing onto furniture or by using the wooden struts that had held the roof up, but were crumbling away. Swein admired their resolve but knew he'd not be doing that, even if it meant Olaf's death. Any moment now he expected the entire roof to collapse.

Above the roaring orange and yellow flames of the hungry fire, Swein caught the eyes of the man he wished dead, expecting to see resignation on his face. Instead Olaf was smirking.

Swein made a movement forward, as if he was going to race towards him, but a hand on his shoulder stopped him and before he could angrily swipe it away, he heard an ominous creek from above his head and watched with horror as one of the roof beams crashed to the floor, taking one of his warriors with it.

For a fleeting moment Swein saw the warrior's anguished face as he realized this meant his death, and then his hair and clothing caught fire and screams of terror burst from his mouth and the sharp tang of burning flesh filled the room as his eyes rolled in his head and his body convulsed in the super heated air, his skin melting from his bones.

Without thought, Swein found himself bellowing 'retreat' as loudly as he could, his eyes fixed on the dying man. As much as he wanted Olaf dead, he didn't want to lose any more of his men to the savage fire.

None of his men deserved such a horrific death, not when they acted on his orders and for his vengeance, not for their own. Swein would have to hope that the fire did the work he now couldn't do without risking his life and that of his followers.

A steady stream of men burst from the blazing hall, their clothing smoldering and the smell of burnt cloth and hair following them. Swein watched them go, frantically trying to ensure that all of his men were accounted for. He hoped that the building remained upright yet, allowing more of his men to scramble to safety.

Swein slowly moved backwards, but his eyes never left the blazing hall, his eyes stinging from the superheated air, but he knew he couldn't leave, not until he knew that Olaf was dead. Swein would stand their until all his men made it to safety and he could be assured that Olaf hadn't managed to somehow evade his trap.

Swein licked his dry lips with anticipation, tasting the salt of the ocean and the iron of death. He hoped his men had managed to detain as many of Olaf's men and ships as possible. There would be a fine treasure for him then and the English king's plans would be in disarray.

Swein turned then to look at the man shouting at him. He couldn't make out his words over the roar of the fire blazing before him, but he followed where he pointed and saw with dismay that through the black night, many of Olaf's ships were managing to paddle their way into the main channel and were making a bid for freedom, their sails back-lit by the glimmer of the moon.

Swein turned his eyes back towards the hall, trying to decide whether or not Olaf was trapped or dead inside the hall. Swein weighed up how much he needed to make sure his errand had succeeded against the mass of men and wealth that were trying to escape.

Swein wanted Long Serpent, Olaf's ship, but didn't know if he wanted it more than he did Olaf.

Swein made a decision.

"Take one of the ships and follow them. I want to know where they go. Then come back here at daybreak and collect me and the rest of the men."

Dryi flashed urgent eyes towards the ships. It was obvious he didn't agree with his decision but neither was he about to admit it, not in public. Instead Dryi turned and grabbing men as he went, made his way towards where Olaf's ships were rapidly trying to leave while Swein's men tried to stop them. Dryi would need to command one of the ships but as Swein's second in command, he'd have no difficulty in having his instructions obeyed.

Another man quickly took his place beside him, and Swein turned his eyes to take in the outraged and annoyed expression on Jarl Sigurd's face. At that moment, Swein almost wished he hadn't sent any warning and that Sigurd had been a victim of the fire as well. It might have been far easier than the conversation he now needed to endure.

For the time being Sigurd simply met his eyes and watched his home burn. Swein hoped Sigurd's thoughts weren't too filled with ideas of how he'd exact revenge for the damage done to him and his family. Swein knew without having to ask that he'd need to pay a hefty price to keep Sigurd's goodwill.

No more men clambered from the burning steading, and up and down its structure, loud cracks and hisses could be heard. The entire upper portion of the building was made of dried grass or wood, the lower of stone. Any moment now Swein felt sure that the whole roof structure would collapse, leaving only the superheated stonework along the base.

Swein idly wondered if it would take long for the structure to cool so that rebuilding work could continue. He hoped not. Winter was snapping at their heels and Sigurd would be greatly displeased if he had no shelter during the cold time of the year.

The night sky was suddenly dark and black, a few clouds obscuring the stars and the moon, and for all the heat from the flames, Swein felt cold. This hadn't been the night's work he'd been expecting it to be.

Swein had anticipated the moment Olaf burst forth from the burning hall and found himself faced with Swein with delight, his hand clenched around his axe, ready to meet the great man face to face. That wasn't going to happen and instead Swein would be known as the man who killed Olaf by burning him alive.

As much as Swein had craved his death, he wasn't sure this act, attached to his name forever, would add to the glory he was trying to build for himself. And there were too many people who'd witnessed these actions for a different story to be concocted.

Anger swelled within him, firmly directed at Olaf.

Then Swein heard a cry from behind the structure and he rushed to see what had so upset the men. When he saw what riled them, he didn't know whether to laugh or to cry.

From the rear of the great hall, a great swirl of smoke and flickering flames leached from the base of the building where a mighty tunnel had been hewn into the stone base of the hall allowing those inside to escape.

Jarl Sigurd followed his rush to the rear of the hall and looked at Swein with raised eyebrows, the gentle shake of Sigurd's head was all Swein needed to know. The tunnel was new. Someone had beaten back the smoke, flames and the grasping weapons of men and had managed to make their own escape route.

Swein knew of only one man strong enough to do such a thing, and if Axe had made the tunnel then he'd have only done it for one person. Axe would rather have died within the flaming hall than live while his war chief died.

Only Axe could have done such a thing and he would only have done it for Olaf.

A small smirk covered Swein's face. Damn, the man wouldn't even die when he wanted him to.

Swein raised his voice,

"Men, spread out, there are survivors, find them."

The dark night was soon lit by an assortment of tiny brands, dipping in and out of every structure that still stood and along the exposed coastline. The animal barn, the sauna, the grain storage, and the homes of the servants and slaves. Everything was searched.

Swein placed his hands on his hips and sighed deeply. It seemed that he had his wish. He'd not be known as the man who burnt Olaf to death. Swein only hoped that they could capture him before he found his ship and made an escape.

Swein gazed towards the beach and thought of Dryi. He hoped he found Olaf on one of the ships.

"So all this and he still lives," Sigurd muttered darkly, his anger evident in his clipped speech but Swein wasn't listening to him. He was trying to think as Olaf would. What would he be doing in this situation? It would depend on whether they had any wounded with them and whether they had the English king's jarl amongst their number.

Swein began to run, some of his men following him, even though he'd issued no commands, as he jumped and sped his way towards where Olaf's ships had beached. The wind rushed past his ears and Swein could hear nothing but the cry of the wind, as though it chastised him for his foolhardy plan.

He should have thought more about what he planned to do, and about how he was going to capture Olaf, but when he'd seen the hall he'd thought only of an immediate end to Olaf.

Swein really should have known better.

Olaf had been an orphan, born after his father's death and yet he'd lived no matter that men had craved his death since he'd taken his first breath. His good luck would have followed him to Shetland. Swein was sure of it.

In the distance Swein hazarded a guess that dawn was close to arriving. The night had passed almost in the blink of an eye and as soon as the sun rose, Olaf would be able to see and find Long Serpent, no matter where she'd hidden, because he was sure the men on board the ship would have done such a thing. They were Olaf's personal warriors, the men he looked to as his protection and he would protect them back.

Swein needed to find the ship before Olaf did.

Cold rain began to sheet from the sky, blurring his vision and making the on-coming sunrise a watery mass that gave little or no light. He had time yet, or so he cautioned himself. He knew he had time yet, provided he could make it to the beach before Olaf did.

As the first pinks of dawn graced the sky, Swein reached the beach where last night he'd known at least thirty ships, maybe more, had been beached and waiting for their crews. Now there was no one left, and more frustratingly, he could see two ships, only just reaching open water. Swein squinted through the rain and the now unwelcome glare of the coming dawn.

Damn. One of the vessels was surely Long Serpent. She was unique and easy to tell apart from all the other ships. Swein watched her go angrily. Olaf yet lived. He knew it for all that he hadn't seen him. Swein knew Olaf's men wouldn't leave without him.

And on the other ship? Swein watched as the sail unfurled and the pit of his stomach turned hollow. He recognized the colours of the sail. He knew who sailed within that ship as it turned and headed towards the open sea.

It could only be the English Jarl.

Swein had hoped to kill an enemy during the nigh. It now appeared that not only had he failed but had more than likely made a new one as well.

Swein cursed angrily inside his head, all the time his expression remaining as neutral as possible as first the rest of his men and then Jarl Sigurd caught up with him.

"My Lord," Jarl Sigurd barked at his back and he was almost tempted to raise his axe and take the man's head from his shoulders for the censor in his voice but now that Olaf was free once more, he needed all the allies he could get.

"Jarl Sigurd?" he said, turning to face the man. He'd need to call on all his patience to deal with the consequences of his hasty actions. He coloured his voice with warmth and remorse in equal measure.

CHAPTER 9
Borgeby, Denmark
AD996

S wein stalked around his hall. He was thinking furiously of the part he needed to play over the next few days.

News of Olaf's survival and his successes in Norway seemed to arrive on every ship that travelled between the lands of Denmark, Sweden and Norway, and with each and every one, his anger grew greater.

News that the English jarl had also survived had only added to his rage. He'd been hoping that the English jarl would die, and the English king would change his mind about his support for Olaf, but he was being denied that hope. It was time to address the problem of Olaf and stop praying that his God, or the old Gods for that matter, would take care of Olaf for him. He was the king, and he needed to act like one.

Firstly he needed allies and with that in mind he'd sent his brother, Haakon, to seek out the mercenary force of the Jomsvikings. He needed men as successful in battle as Olaf, men who seemed to carry the luck of their Gods with them. Haakon was due to return soon and in the meantime Swein was playing host to Olof Skötkonung, the new king of Sweden, and his stepson. They were uneasy allies. It was Olof who'd tried to claim his throne when he was in England, Ireland and Shetland and it was Olof who Swein had beaten away from his shores on his return. His brother had done well in his absence and Olof, and he had reached an accord but it was an uneasy one, and it needed to be continually reaffirmed.

While he was growing fond of his stepson's mother, he couldn't say the same about his stepson. He was very young to be a king, and he was even more awkward than Swein had ever been. He found Olof tested his patience with his strange ideas and his confidence in his abilities. He was almost as insufferable as his enemy, Olaf of Norway. The only advantage was that Swein was still a better and more seasoned commander than Olof would ever be. It was Olof's father's legacy that kept his men loyal and as Swein knew only too well, relying on what fathers had done before wasn't always the ideal way to rule. Sons were not their fathers and fathers, not their sons. He wondered how long it would take the men of Sweden to realise that.

He'd agreed to meet Olof at Borgeby in Skane. It gave him the opportunity to check on the building work at his Trelleborg fortress and also meant that Olof wasn't close to mainland Denmark. Swein didn't want to put temptation in front of him. He'd made no secret of his desire to take Denmark away from Swein, just as his predecessor had tried to do before him. It was far better to be his ally than his enemy. He was planning on working harder to keep Olof friendlier than he'd ever managed with Olaf. Not that he thought it was any easier. It was just what he needed to do.

Borgeby was almost complete, and he was proud of his fortress. It might have been his father's decision to build the Trelleborg fortresses, but he'd capitalised on the idea, and he now had four completed fortifications and a further two either nearing completion or in the planning stages. They'd been invaluable when he'd decided to attack England because he'd had men trained and ready to take with him. It wasn't their fault that their expedition had been so monumentally unsuccessful. No, it was Olaf's fault for providing bad information and for trying to accomplish something that even their ancestors hadn't managed – a concerted attack on London to exact a huge sum of tribute.

He thought Borgeby was an apt place to make a show of his

strength to young Olof, and his own sons were accompanying him as was his new wife. He'd planned a great feast, and he hoped to overawe Olof with his organisational skills and his show of force and wealth.

His wife, Sigrid, sat before the blazing fire, an amused expression on her face as she watched her younger husband's pacing. She was a clever woman, skilled in politics and intrigue and Swein, despite himself, was grudgingly accepting of her. That she was also a delight in bed helped the situation they found themselves in. It was, after all, a marriage of convenience to seal an alliance. They were not always the most successful.

A commotion from outside and the door to the hall opened, and Olof stepped inside, surrounded by some of his own men, and also other men that Swein didn't recognise but thought he had a fair idea of whom they were. Was it possible that Olof had already made an alliance with the Jomsvikings?

Sigrid quietly chuckled as she watched her son and Swein quirked a smile as well. It was typical that Olof was one step ahead of him when he'd thought himself so far thinking. Only then his brother strode into the room as well, and suddenly it wasn't so obvious who was allied with whom.

Swein stepped forward and embraced his stepson. He'd gained bulk since they'd last met. Olof planned on being a great warrior, and he was flanked by at least ten men in full war gear. He might have come to discuss peace and an alliance, but he did so making his warlike inclinations clear.

Swein called for drink and food and indicated that the men should seat themselves with his own men and then, as Olof went to greet his mother, he walked towards his brother. Haakon seemed amused by the interplay of characters meeting in one place, and Swein felt a little overwhelmed as well.

As Olof hadn't introduced the other men to him, he raised an eyebrow at Haakon.

"Brother," he said, "I've reached an accord with the Jomsvikings, and I've brought their representatives to negotiate with you. This King Swein, is Thorkell, known as the tall, as I'm sure you can appreciate."

Haakon had become a poised man. He was confident of his position with his brother, and he knew that he had the power to act alone, and also in his brother's name. Still, it seemed as though the Jomsvikings needed some further assurances from the king himself. Swein was happy to make those guarantees. With Olof and Thorkell in his hall, he almost felt as though he had a firm alliance against Olaf. All that remained was for his other ally, Erik of Lade, to make his appearance.

"King Swein," the large Jomsviking said, reaching out to grasp the arm of Swein and in the process draw attention to the large number of arm rings that decorated his own arm. Thorkell was, it appeared, one of the most successful of the men.

"Thorkell, it's good to meet with you."

"And you King Swein," the large man continued, his eyes roving over the hall they were within. "This is a mighty fortress you have here. I'm pleased I entered it as an ally and not an enemy."

Swein inclined his head to accept the compliment for what it was.

"And I'm pleased you're here as my ally and not my enemy. Come, drink with me. Meet my wife and sons."

They made their way towards the raised platform where his wife and his sons were watching the visitors with curious eyes. Swein smirked to see the awe on his young son's faces. They were too young to be surrounded by warriors, but at the same time, Swein firmly believed that they needed to learn how to rule even now. They should watch, as he once had, and they needed to admire men who might play them false so that they learnt the bitter taste of betrayal.

"Sigrid, Harald, Cnut, this is Thorkell, of the Jomsvikings."

While Sigrid clearly knew Thorkell, both of his sons had heard such fantastical tales of the Jomsvikings that they both inadvertently took a step backwards.

"Harald, Cnut, I'm pleased to meet the sons of the great Swein of Denmark." Thorkell's voice boomed even in the great hall. Swein thought the boys might be overawed but Cnut, his youngest stepped forward and solemnly held his arm out to greet the huge warrior. He had pale blond hair and fragile looking eyes, but he had a firm resolve that more than made up for his physical lack.

Thorkell grasped Cnut's arm gently but formally, and Swein knew his first moment of pride in the boy.

It took Harald a few moments to recover from his initial shock and his younger brother's forthrightness, but he too stepped forward and introduced himself to the great giant of a man. Swein ruffled their heads in pride and even his new wife looked impressed by the boys, the one blond, the other dark despite the fact they shared a mother and a father. For all that Sigrid's own son wasn't the finest specimen Swein had ever met, she was often critical of his sons. He was pleased now that she'd have to reconsider her assessment of them.

Haakon joined them on the raised platform and then they all moved to a long board laid out with food and a great feast began. Swein had invited as many of his men as he could fit inside the hall and they mingled with the Jomsvikings Thorkell had with him and the Swedish men they already knew because of their earlier encounters with Olof.

Swein planned for the feast to take all night, and he'd arranged for a skald to entertain them later. He wanted to present himself as the great and mighty king that he was and then come the morning, he and Olof, and now Thorkell could discuss their intentions towards Olaf. He almost wished the feast done with, or that he'd held the talks before the feast. He was impatient to know that the men would help him attack Olaf.

The news from Trondheim was that Olaf had made landfall, had been accepted by men and women who'd known his father or who'd hated the now dead king and begun the conversion to Christianity that had been a part of his treaty with the English king. The last trader who'd been intercepted by Swein before he'd journeyed to Borgeby had mentioned that Olaf had the help of English priests and had begun work on a wooden church. Swein thought that Olaf was making far too much of his recent baptism at the hands of the English king, but it was pointless to moan and complain that Olaf had long been a Christian. No one seemed to hear the truth only the growing legend of the man.

Swein knew that there was still much resistance to Olaf's rule, and he'd made it very clear that he'd offer support to anyone who rose in rebellion against Olaf. He hoped that soon he'd have even more allies to eat at his board and drink his mead.

The feast was long and fruitful, the skald regaling them all with tales of the Old Gods and occasionally straying into new stories as told by the men and women who'd decided to make their home on the new Iceland far to the north. Swein could understand the pull of new land. If he'd not been a king, he'd have wanted to be a freeman, answerable to no one.

The mead flowed and so too did the songs of daring deeds and soon Swein found himself alone with a very drunk Olof and a slightly more sober Thorkell. His wife had long since sought her bed, and his sons slept where they'd fallen asleep, their heads resting on folded arms on the board before them. Swein felt sure that the noise of the men would wake them, but so far they'd not stirred at all.

Haakon was awake as well, but his eyes were unfocused. He'd drunk far too much to be useful.

"So my Lord Swein," Thorkell began, "I think we should speak of Olaf now while the majority of the men and women sleep. Your vendetta, it's a personal one?"

Swein glared at Thorkell's censorship. Personal vendettas were the only ones that mattered.

"He made a fool of me, risked my men in combat against the English and then when I tried to kill him, he escaped and made himself King of Norway."

"You could just say yes my Lord," Thorkell spoke drily. "The men of the Jomsvikings prefer it if the men who want to pay them to fight tell the truth."

Swein considered that and nodded.

"Agreed, then yes, it is a personal vendetta. He was supposed to be my ally, but he merely endangered my men and made an alliance with the English as soon as I'd left England and he must die for that. He thinks he's a king, but he's not. The land he claims in Norway belongs to another, and I would support the other man over Olaf."

Olof smirked to hear his stepfather being spoken to so abruptly, but he held his tongue. He thought Olaf was a menace that needed containing as well.

"The Jomsvikings will help you, never fear. I believe that you have enough men and enough support already, but you're right to be cautious. Olaf has the reputation of one of the old Gods, and he uses it to great effect even though he now follows the new Christian God. He has many allies, or he had many allies. He stands virtually alone now that he claims a kingdom. It should be easy to arrange a battle against him and ensure he dies."

Olof giggled drunkenly to hear Thorkell speak so matter of factly about killing men.

"Thorkell, you've changed little since I first met you," he hiccupped, "you think only of other men's deaths and never your own."

Thorkell's eyes narrowed a little as he looked at the young king.

"You'd do well to learn from my example," he simply said before turning back to Swein.

"The Jomsvikings will want payment and perhaps land from you. I would like to suggest a Trelleborg fort such as this, but I understand that would be too great a prize. I will think about it, and so will my fellow Jomsvikings. But know this, if we join with you, we'll expect to have a say on what you plan and how you intend to carry it out. We will not blindly go where you leave."

Swein considered that. It seemed a small thing to barter.

"You have my word," he said, offering a handclasp to seal their bargain.

"And you have mine," Thorkell responded.

Olof too reached out and joined the men, and so did Haakon, the four of them wrapping their hands around each other.

And just like that, Swein had his alliance.

Now all he needed was the opportunity to attack Olaf.

It couldn't come soon enough.

CHAPTER 10
The Battle of Svoldor
AD999

S wein watched the chill waters as though daring them to grow torrid with the threat of the coming storm. It was a cold day on the sea. He knew on land near about it was far warmer and far more pleasant. He shivered a little, the threat of the coming winter worried him more than the coming battle. It made him reassess himself, and he almost liked what he found.

Olaf had been an unsteady ally, not always reliable and not always much of an ally. It had proved far easier to think like that, in the end, he'd been an enemy all along and never an ally.

He regretted that he'd not managed to kill him on Shetland, but he blamed the damn fool Englishman for that. He shouldn't have bloody been there in the first place. He should have been at home licking England's wounds and making more gold and silver for the Vikings. He shouldn't have been attempting to meddle in the affairs of the Danish kingdom and those that surrounded her, and if he'd not been there, Olaf, Axe and his men would have been more concerned with revenge than protecting the English jarl.

He pulled his cloak tighter around his body as he remembered the attack on Shetland. He'd felt confident that his men had killed Olaf. He'd been bitterly disappointed when he'd discovered that not only had Olaf escaped. He'd also managed to claim the Norwegian kingdom just as he'd always dreamed of doing.

It had taken four more long years to assemble an alliance against him. Once he was home in Norway, the task of killing him had become far more challenging, and he'd known that unless he'd employed an assassin, it would have been impossible to do. The thought of an assassin had made his blood run a little cold. It was one thing to kill a man in the heat of battle, or while he was sheltered by an ally, but an assassin? No, there would have been no honour in using an assassin to kill him. Bad enough that everyone knew he'd tried to burn Olaf to death. He didn't want others to know that he'd even considered using an assassin, let alone used one.

Now he stood on the prow of his ship, as he had done throughout the last two days and he waited for Olaf to make an appearance.

It was a dull and tedious task but one that needed doing all the same. Olaf had slipped past his lookouts on his way to the land of his first wife, Wendland, but he would not be sneaking back again.

No, Swein honestly hoped that this time Olaf did meet his death, and if possible on the edge of his blade.

His allies, Olof and Erik, were content to wait as well. Neither of them wanted Olaf to have any more success. He was already far too powerful. If he'd been successful in Wendland as well, he'd be unstoppable.

"He'll come, my Lord," a voice drifted from inside his ship, and Swein grinned to hear Thorkell's calm voice. They'd become friends in the aftermath of the English raid. So unlike his and Olaf's relationship.

"I wish he'd bloody get on with it," Swein huffed in annoyance. Thorkell chuckled at the angry tone.

"When have you ever known anything you wanted happen when you wanted it to?"

Swein didn't answer. Thorkell was correct in his summation. Still, it didn't make the waiting any easier.

He watched his allies, for want of anything better to do. Of the two men, it was Olof that he knew the least about and the one he was most wary off.

He'd brought fifteen ships along to their enterprise and Swein knew that for that he expected to get great rewards. Swein hoped that Olaf had managed to gather together the great wealth he'd often joked about being buried in Wendland. Much of his wealth was consolidated in the trelleborg's he'd continued to build and fill. He didn't want to have to use any of his own carefully hoarded treasures to pay off Olof if their alliance against Olaf proved to be unsuccessful.

Not that it would. This time, he had every confidence in himself. This time, Olaf would lose his life and Swein would gain his wealth. It made the long, cold wait worthwhile.

Erik was a much closer personal friend of Swein's. He'd needed no manipulating at all to join the alliance and had brought twenty-five ships to the coming battle, leaving Swein as the dominant power with thirty-five ships and the most to lose if they missed Olaf or by some miracle, he lived through the attack. Erik had commented that their numbers were a little like over-kill as rumour had it that Olaf sailed with only ten ships. He'd expected no trouble when he set out for Wendland and had been far more concerned with holding his land in Norway than in protecting himself. He'd left the bulk of his warriors in Trondheim.

Swein believed that their attack would once and for all wipe the smirk of delight off Olaf's lips. He hoped he'd be the man to kill him but didn't much care provided he ended up dead by the end of the battle.

The chill day slowly drew to a close and still there was no sign of Olaf's fleet on the dipping waters. Lanterns were affixed to the ships, to beat the dark back; they looked like tiny stars only far closer to his land than normal. Still, Olaf didn't come.

Stiff and tired from his day of standing Swein finally relinquished his position at the front of the ship and beckoned Dyri to take his place. Dyri kept the groan from his voice, but Swein knew that he'd just been gifted the most unenvied role on their expedition. The men were already tired from their inactivity and cold from waiting on the sea's cooling waters. Watch duty during the night on a gently swaying ship was a lesson in alertness that few ever mastered. The amount of times that Swein himself had almost slept the night away was all the proof he needed of that.

Some of the other men called out congratulations or commiserations as Dyri passed Swein on his way to the front of the ship.

"Keep alert, I think he may try and sneak past us," he grunted as he sought his own space to fall asleep in on the compact vessel.

The words proved to be an apt warning as Swein was raised from his deep sleep to a slate blue sky, the possibility of dawn still some way off and the whispered words of Dyri.

"He's trying to sneak past. I think he has eleven ships, and they're all trying to row past us. It was only the muffled cough of a man that alerted me to their presence."

Swein nodded in the gloom as he listened hard through the stillness of the early day to see if Dyri was correct in his conclusions.

He strained his ears and heard nothing at all for long, long moments over the slap of the water against his ship, but then he too detected the scuff of an oar on the flat surface. Dryi looked at him for confirmation and Swein nodded vigorously to show that he'd heard it as well and Dryi didn't imagine things.

Quickly he sent Dyri to steal down the ship and wake their men. Ideally, he would have preferred to alert the other ships he commanded, but he didn't want Olaf to know what he was doing. He'd have to hope that they woke and were ready for action as soon as he raised the alarm. They'd been warned, just as Dyri had, that he thought Olaf would sneak past them during one of the nights. Olof and Erik had been warned as well.

If only he could use the power of thought to wake them, but that was impossible.

His men sprang to life as quickly and quietly as they could. Their weapons had been wrapped in leathers or cloths to protect them from the harsh elements of the sea and Swein grimaced as he heard the metals being removed and made ready.

Being silent was impossible. He even imagined that he could listen to the heartbeats of the men as they worked.

He remained where he was, straining his ears to hear any telltale sign of where the ships were. He had no idea how Dyri had reasoned that Olaf had eleven ships. He could see next to nothing beyond a few sword lengths in front of him. He was thinking frantically. It was hard enough to envisage a battle on the open sea; it was even more difficult to imagine one while it was still dark.

The small light from the lanterns was not sufficient to see by. Should he force a confrontation now or wait and follow Olaf until daylight stole over the sea? He knew waiting was the right action to take, but he could feel his impatience rising, his ire at being made to wait so long for Olaf to appear threatened to make him act irrationally. It was evident that Olaf had known that Swein had gathered together a force against him and that he'd waited until the darkest time of the month, when the moon was completely hidden, to try and make his escape. Swein couldn't quite believe the arrogance of the man.

He calmed himself. He would imperil his own men if he tried to fight now. No one would be able to see to balance on the ships, and that would mean that his far superior numbers would be a hindrance.

He thought quickly. He'd have to follow Olaf until dawn and get word to the other ships of his intentions. He would need them with him when the fighting began. Dyri was back by now, and he whispered to him what he thought they should do. Thorkell had joined them as well, his eyes were bright and alert, flashing dangerously in the pale light from the lantern.

"I'll swim to the other ships my Lord," he offered almost immediately and Swein shivered at the thought of it. The water was frigid.

Thorkell grinned when he felt the shiver ripple through the ship.

"It's only cold if you think it is," he offered, and Swein smirked at the challenge in his voice.

"However you can convince yourself you'll survive is fine with me, but that would be a good idea. Ensure Erik knows. We'll follow the ships."

Thorkell was already divesting himself of his heavy clothes, removing his byrnie and his weapons. It would be a waste if he sank without a trace because he failed to realise he couldn't swim with all his equipment.

Dyri was watching Thorkell with shock.

"My Lord?" he said to Swein and Swein patted him on the shoulder.

"Don't worry Dyri. Thorkell swims like a seal. He'll survive."

Swein shared Dyri's shock about Thorkell's intentions. The men might well spend all their days on board a ship but the thought of swimming through the waters their ships sat upon was not a pleasant one. He appreciated that Dyri was probably a weak swimmer. The idea that they might need to swim was a strange one for his men to comprehend. After all, the ship was there so that they didn't need to swim.

With a cheery wave, Thorkell lowered himself into the water silently, as though he truly was a creature of the sea, and Swein, happy to see all his men now armed and ready to row, passed along whispered instructions to his men. They were to row, and he would direct them. They weren't to row too quickly, and if the man in front stopped rowing, then they were to do the same. That way Swein only had to get a message to the two lead oarsmen.

Still, in the dark and gloom of the early morning, Swein set out with his one ship to track Olaf's moves. For a moment he worried that it might all be a trap but he pushed the thought aside. Olaf was a sneaky bastard but for once he thought he was just trying to escape himself and that any thoughts of retribution against Swein, Erik or Olof were far from his mind.

They'd been sheltering as close to the shore as they could get without actually beaching the ships, and now Swein was surprised by the force of the wind that buffeted his ship as it slowly moved out from the shelter the land had been providing. He pulled his sea cloak tighter around himself, grateful for the seal-skin that allowed the water to slope from him when it impacted against him.

His hands were encased in gloves as well, but he knew his face, where it was exposed to the wind's chill, would be red and glowing before too long. His eyes also stung from the cold.

It was the summer, and yet an icy spell had gripped the region. He wasn't surprised that Olaf had decided now was the time to return home. He must have been trying to get home before the first winter storms struck.

Swein intended to ensure that didn't happen.

His hearing was so attuned to the sounds of the stealthy ships that he was beginning to make out more and more of the noise. He could hear the slap of the oars over the sea, for all that it was being done as quietly as possible, and he fancied he could also hear the men whispering to each other. He strained even further but he didn't hear Olaf's voice warning the men that they were being pursued but he did listen to the sound of more ships following him.

He grinned. Thorkell and his foolhardy idea to swim between the stationary ships had apparently worked. He imagined that by the time the sun lit the horizon enough for them to be able to see by, all of his ships would be arranged against Olaf's, and he'd have a very nasty shock.

Now he just needed to hope that Olaf and his men didn't have their sail hoisted and that the wind didn't pick up. If that happened, he'd lose valuable time hoisting his own sail.

The chase went on for what felt like a long time. Swein was beginning to think that some terrible event had befallen the sun and it was never going to rise again. The semi-light didn't even seem to be growing, and he curbed his impatience once more. Always his downfall he began praying to his God and asking him to hurry the sunrise. He wanted the battle to start sooner rather than later.

Then, when he almost thought that his fanciful thoughts had made the day stay dark and clouded, he saw a faint burst of sunlight ahead and knew that day would soon be upon them. He looked forward hungrily, hoping to see Olaf's ships, but was met with nothing but a smudge on the horizon. No matter how much he squinted he could see nothing, the sea still painted in the colours of the night despite the streak of purple stretching across the sky. He cursed and then he cursed once more.

A shot of sunlight glistened in the sky, and he heard a gasp of outrage from behind him before he ducked to avoid the flaming missile in the air. He heard it hit the sea and sizzle as the flame died, but he knew that Olaf now knew he was there. He shouted to his men, demanding they speed up and catch up with the fleeing men. There was no longer any need for caution.

As he did so, he glanced behind him and saw with relief that there was a whole host of ships racing to catch him, their night lanterns no longer extinguished. By his estimations, most of the ships had heeded the commands of Thorkell and were chasing Olaf.

He grinned with the anticipation of the coming battle, and then ducked as Dyri's shout caught his ear. Another flaming arrow was bearing down on his ship. He watched with interest to see if this one would reach its intended mark. It didn't, but it was a close thing, and he still couldn't see Olaf's ships or where the arrows were coming from. The sea was cast in dark shadows. If he'd let his imagination run wild, he could almost have thought that the old sea god was trying to attack him. But he knew Olaf was there, endeavouring to avoid them.

He called for Molti. He was the most skilled with an arrow of all the men.

"Molti, can you fire back at them?"

Molti didn't even consider the question. He'd brought his bow and arrow to the prow of the ship with him and was eyeing the lit swinging lantern, trying to decide what he could use to make his arrow flame as it flew.

Swein was considering the same, and he reached for the bundle of cloth they carried with them and tore long strips from what should have been an expensive and bright blue bolt of fabric but which was going to do little more than act as a means to try and set Olaf's own ships on fire. He didn't even take the time to consider how much wealth he was literally burning. He reached for a wooden jug and poured strong ale over the cloth to make it burn.

Molti quickly realised what Swein was doing, and they worked together to wrap the cloth around the end of one of the arrows. Then Molti readied himself, trying to plant his feet and make himself steady on the swaying ship that now dashed through the gentle sea, sending a very thin plume of spray all over the men inside the ship.

He too couldn't see where Olaf's man was aiming from, but he waited and waited, hoping for another flaming missile to come their way so that he could point directly at where the arrow originated.

Swein glared at the lax sunrise. Why would the sun not rise? It would make his task so much easier. Then he thought of Thorkell's words the day before and shrugged his shoulders. He was right. Nothing he wanted had ever been as easy to achieve as he'd hoped it would be, not even removing his father from power. That should have been easy enough to accomplish, but his father had fought back with such passion that only his death had rectified the situation.

A flash caught his eye and in the same moment, Molti set fire to and sent back his own burning arrow. In the ark of the streaming light, Swein caught the first glimpse of Olaf's ships, and he swallowed back a stab of fear.

Olaf had pulled his ships together in a parody of a shield wall. Five ships stretched across the sea in front of him, with another five behind them, and then a spare ship to the rear. Swein assumed it was the reserve force, intended to reinforce wherever there was a breach in the defence.

But what worried him most were the men with bows and arrow. He had Molti who was proficient with the bow and arrow but other than that, most of the men were more skilled in the weapons of the shield wall. Even spears were problematic in the confined space of the ships. It was just as easy to kill your enemy as to knock your ally backwards into the sea. He knew because he and his men had been training for this sea battle for much of the summer. He'd known that this was the year to kill Olaf, and he'd hazarded the hope that they'd intercept him on one of his many sea voyages. That was why it galled so much that he'd managed

SWEIN: THE DANISH KING

to sneak past them without being noticed. He needed to make amends for that now.

Molti's arrow landed short, but it gave him enough of an idea of Olaf's intentions. He might well have tried to return to Norway without notice, but he must have decided when that failed, that he'd stand and fight where he was. He'd given considerable thought to his formation, so similar to the one in London and yet also very different, and Swein once more appreciated what a formidable opponent he really was.

He would not be easy to kill, but then, he never had been. He was a lucky man. Following his father's death at the hands of King Olof's father, the fact that he'd survived to adulthood had been a tremendous feat. To live long enough to make himself a king was another one.

The men in his ship kept to their positions, rowing slowly towards Olaf's few ships. They looked insignificant across the vast expanse of the grey sea. Swein looked behind him and saw that Erik had forced his ship close to his own and that Olof was doing the same thing. The men looked determined and surprised in equal measure as the sun finally lifted above the horizon and illuminated Olaf's attempt to thwart their attack. Swein could see Thorkell on Erik's ship, and he was pleased to find his friend unharmed from his immersion in the water.

"Swein," Erik bellowed from his ship. The need for silence was well and truly past. "What do you plan?" he demanded, his voice clipped. He was assessing the ships, trying to look for weaknesses to exploit. The biggest one that Swein could see was the gaping space behind Olaf's few ships.

"Someone should go around the back, cut off his retreat."

Erik nodded and Olof came to join the discussion.

"I want to attack him from the front," the taciturn man said and Swein held his annoyance in place. Olof was a man of little compromise. He liked everything to be his own way. That was one of the reasons that Swein found their alliance so difficult. Of course the other was that Swein's wife was the man's stepmother. That almost made them family. Almost.

"I'll lead my men around the back," Erik said, cutting off Swein's mildly angry retort. Olof was setting himself up for the greater victory.

Another arrow coloured the dawn with it's flaming orange and yellow, and Olof ducked unconsciously, even though the arrow was too far away to impact the vessel. Erik grinned, but Olof didn't see, and Swein tried to keep his face neutral.

"I'll split my men and attack the left and the right," Swein said into the silence, and Olof shot him an annoyed look. He didn't like the thought of his men being surrounded. Swein huffed on his anger. The man needed to decide what was more important, being the one to kill Olaf or trusting his allies?

A tense moment passed, and Swein was aware of activity on Olaf's ships. He wondered what they were planning now. He squinted at the ships. They were fully visible, and Swein could tell that they were weighed down with great treasures because the ships were low in the water. The oars on the side that faced his ships had been brought on board and stowed away. Swein thought it a bad decision because it would allow his ships to get closer without being impeded by them. He couldn't believe that Olaf would be so stupid as to give the opposition an advantage, but he supposed the Norwegian King might well be desperate in the face of such unbalanced odds.

Erik nodded in agreement and Olof finally gave his grudging assent to the plan.

"Are we just going to attack?" Erik asked when no one made a move to order the three neighbouring ships to move.

"No, I think we should send some more of the fire arrows first," Swein offered. He'd been considering this. It was one thing to march or run to a shield wall, quite another to face the same on the sea. It was a calm day as the sun stole its way along the grey sea, illuminating it and removing its forbidding nature as it passed over it. But men who faced the wall of shields on the sides of Olaf's ships would still be risking certain death at the bottom of the sea should they fight with their heavy byrnies and with all their weapons. Olaf had his shields menacingly locked together along the side of the ships that faced them. Swein was sure he'd employed the same technique on the side he couldn't see.

Swein was considering removing his own byrnie but keeping his shield and his helm; he hoped that if he were then tipped into the sea, he'd be able to let go of his shield and remove his helm. He was also thinking about leaving his weapons belt behind. After all, how many weapons did he need? A seax or a sword or an axe would be enough.

Apart from the stray fire arrows he saw, he couldn't make out how any of Olaf's men were armed, but he knew that the warrior would have a technique he'd not considered. That should worry him, but he was hoping that their sheer numbers would overawe them, provided they were able to get close enough to let their numbers speak for themselves.

Erik glanced at him then, already shrugging his own metaled byrnie from his shoulders.

"I'm ordering my men to remove their vests," he said, " I don't want them to drown. The weight of the metal is bad enough, without water being added."

"I'm going to do the same," Swein said, but he could already see Thorkell and Dyri following Erik's example. He wished they weren't doing it quite so openly. Olaf was sure to see what they were doing and instruct his men to take advantage of their lack of protection. He would instruct the archer to aim at men's chests, knowing full well that provided he hit his mark, the men would be severely wounded.

Olof looked unimpressed at the activity, and in fact tightened his own weapons belt and circled his arms to ensure he had the most movement he could achieve from his own byrnie.

"My men can choose as they will," he muttered, his gaze never straying from where Olaf's ships waited patiently. The amount of time they'd been discussing tactics, Olaf could easily have made his own escape, but he'd decided to fight. Swein was growing impatient.

"We just attack. Get the men ready. Erik, as soon as you reach the side of the shield wall, I'm going to call my men to attack, you should do the same Olof."

Swein fixed Erik with a knowing look, and the pair glared at Olof, who was licking his lips, whether with nerves or anticipation Swein was unsure. He didn't want Olof to be the man to kill Olaf, but he needed to at least give him the opportunity. As soon as the battle was underway, he'd get Thorkell and Dryi to help him fight his way to Olaf's side. He needed to make the killing blow. Only then would he know that the man was indeed dead.

The three ships finally rowed themselves apart, and Swein gave his instructions to the commanders of the other thirty-four ships he commanded. Not every ship was to enter the fray. He wanted the majority to hold off unless it looked as though Olaf was going to escape or they were going to sink or lose the battle.

The men looked at him with knowing eyes. The commanders knew what the death of Olaf meant to Swein. Some had been very outspoken in their unhappiness that he'd involved Olof and he was aware that others were hoping and praying that he too would lose his life in the coming battle. Some of his men were more land-hungry than he was. Those were the men he allowed to command his ships and hold control in his trelleborg's. They could be too aggressive, but sometimes aggression was what was needed.

The sun had fully risen by now, and Swein could see all he needed to see, apart from Olaf or in fact any of his men. A sudden fear had him wondering if Olaf had perhaps set the ships this way and then allowed his men to slip their way into the remaining ships and they even now paddled furiously away. Then another flaming arrow shot through the sky, and he knew that Olaf was waiting to face him, as arrogant in his belief that he'd beat him as Swein was in his.

Erik's ships were rowing into position, and Swein was ready to give the command to advance when a hot flaming arrow shot from the five ships, all aimed at Erik's ships. He watched in shock as at least some of the arrows reached their target while other's disappeared harmlessly into the sea. He turned to his own archer and counted how many arrows he had at his disposal. Not enough, that was for sure.

The cries of the men on the five ships that were alight reached his ears, and he winced. Only one or two of the arrow managed to catch on flammable materials inside the ships, but that was all it took. The ships stopped in their tracks and men shouted angrily to each other to put the flames out. All the time, more and more arrows bombarded them.

Swein could see Erik frantically trying to bring some order to the ships on the left-hand side of Olaf while to the right, unnoticed until almost the last moment, Olaf's roaming ship moved to intercept the other half of his fleet. Swein had seen enough.

"Attack," he shouted at the top of his voice, and his select ships shot forward, their crews of sixty men powering through the water. He directed his ship to collide with the vessel that was as far to the left as possible. He was close to Erik and hoped that the men from the ships that burnt would be able to reach the safety of his own vessel, but he was more focused on capsizing Olaf's ships. He wanted Erik's men to see his ship as a lifesaver and Olaf's men to see it as a life taker.

His ship cut through the waves without any problems, and almost before the men had settled into a steady rowing rhythm he was bracing himself for the impact. The silence of the early morning chase had evaporated now that battle was nearly upon them. He held tight to his axe. After careful thought, he'd decided it was the most versatile weapon. He'd be able to use it to force the shields from the side of the ship, and he'd also be able to force holes into the bottom of the ships if he decided he needed to sink them. His byrnie had been passed to one of the ships that were hovering near the back of the attack, along with his more elaborate shield and weapons. For this bloody engagement, he needed nothing but a beaten and worn shield and an axe. Anything else was more likely to bring about his death rather than Olaf's.

He offered a swift pray to his God and then his ship impacted with Olaf's vessel. The sound of wood hitting wood rippled through his vessel as shards of timber shot over his head. He covered his head with his shield and waited a moment for the initial effect of the collision to settle. His ship had tried to rear above Olaf's own, and he knew he would have to jump down into the enemy vessel. He'd not foreseen that difficulty until now.

Unaware of anything around him, he removed his shield and looked for the first time at Olaf's men. The ship was bristling with weapons. As his own ship settled onto Olaf's, it was impaled by spears that tried to force holes into the bottom of it. While the shields of the men that had been neatly stowed away down the side of the ship slowly gave way, one at a time, forcing his own vessel to settle unevenly, in stages that dropped the men to their knees. He tried to step forward, but as he did his ship buckled and he was forced to his knees.

The men behind him let out cries of unhappiness at the strange movement, and for a brief flicker of time, Swein felt as though he had the power to fly. The ship finally settled on top of Olaf's own and he looked for the best way to jump down into the other ship. Only there was no need. Some of Olaf's men had taken advantage of Swein's ships unusual movement to clamber on board, hauling themselves up and over the sides of the ship with their own axes or hands.

Swein hefted his axe. This wasn't going at all as he'd planned it when he'd envisaged a battle at sea.

The first warrior came before him, his eyes flashing ice blue, his teeth gritted in a growl of anger, and Swein was almost too slow to stop the movement of his massive axe. At the last possible moment, he managed to get his shield between him and the axe while behind him he watched Thorkell run his own axe across the man's exposed neck. Blood spurted abruptly, covering his face and temporarily blinding him.

"My thanks," he called, but Thorkell was already looking for his next target.

Swein bent down and hefted the weight of the massive axe his first enemy had held. He wasn't sure if he'd be able to swing it, or even if he wanted to, but it was better for the weapon to be in his hands than in any of Olaf's men.

To the side of him, Thorkell was engaged in a fierce battle with a powerful warrior, his face set in the grimace of combat, and up and down his ship the rest of his men were doing the same. He wanted to make his way to the enemy craft, but he worried that it would sink with the weight of his ship forcing it down. Already water was pooling over its side where his ship rested on the shield wall. The ship had been riding low in the water as it was and now it was even lower. But there was nothing for it. If he wanted to get to Olaf, who he could hear fighting along the length of the ships, he needed to move from his own ship.

He took a breath wondering if his death was written in the stars for today and then calling to Dryi he jumped down into a small space that had opened up where his ship crisscrossed with the enemy one. For a moment nothing happened, and then he felt the timbers below his feet give ever so slightly. Panic turned his legs heavy, but he looked about him and quickly clambered away from the weak point, shouting to Dryi to watch where he went.

The air was filled with the sound of shield and axe, sword and arrow, spear and seax and the unmistakable noise of men tumbling overboard, possibly to never be seen again. A watery death was supposed to be peaceful. Swein doubted it and didn't wish it for himself.

Dryi followed him as he dodged to avoid the fights already ongoing between his own men and Olaf's. He was too caught up in the heat of the battle to know what was happening around him, but he heard the unmistakable sound of an arrow heading his way and ducked behind his shield. He imagined Olaf had the man focused exclusively on where he walked. He'd hoped his lack of distinctive war gear would hinder Olaf's identification of him, but he was obviously wrong.

A man barred his path, his hair all gone to grey and a smile of malice on his face. Swein stopped his mad dash forward and examined the man. Axe. He was almost as good a kill as Olaf was.

"Swein," he said, bowing his head a little, even though all around him fires raged and men fought for their lives. Swein couldn't help himself. He grinned at the warrior's refined manners.

"Axe, it's not good to see you, but then, you know that."

"I do my Lord yes. I'd hoped that one day you'd see the error of your ways and fight side by side with Olaf but clearly that's never going to happen. Olaf has personally given me permission to ensure you die well."

Swein swallowed his fear at those words. Axe was a formidable warrior. He held an axe even longer and heavier in his hands than the one that his first opponent had possessed, the one that Swein had been unsure about carrying, and Axe hefted it as though it weighed no more than a newborn babe. If he faced Axe, he'd need to ensure that he fought precisely and killed him quickly. He'd not be able to fend off a fierce attack from him for long, not with his old shield.

"And I would very much prefer to give you the honour, but today is the day you meet your death, not I."

Axe grinned at that, licking his lips with anticipation and flexing his muscles as he swung the axe around his head.

"We shall see my Lord," he offered, before taking one step backwards and then turning into his first attack. Swein was expecting it but even so, the force behind the blow surprised him, and he took a step backwards, pleased to hear Thorkell at his back. Thorkell and Axe were old enemies as well, and Swein hoped that Thorkell would distract the giant man and so enable him to press on with his wish to kill Olaf.

As if hearing his thoughts, Thorkell wormed his way between him and Axe's attack and as much as Axe wanted to attack Swein he found himself caught in a more evenly matched encounter. Swein moved out of the way, being careful not to misstep in the confined space. Men were busy attacking all around him, and everyone needed one eye on their opponent and one eye on where they next stood.

Swein eyed the distance between this ship and the next one along. Olaf was another ship away yet, and another of Swein's ships had crashed into this one. It had made less of an impact than his own ship, and yet he still needed to tread carefully. Molti was beside him, and he hoped he'd stay with him until Thorkell killed Axe and made his way to join them as well.

He gauged the distance between the two vessels and leapt between them. It wasn't so much that they weren't next to each other, more that the ship his own vessel had crashed into was half sunk and water was lapping over its edges in a menacing way. Swein knew that one missed step would see him getting a frigid bath.

The hiss of an arrow beside his head made him raise his shield, and he felt the arrow impact and smelt the tang of the leather as it burnt. Olaf's archer had sent a fire arrow his way. He felt his anger rising. Bad enough to die from an arrow wound, worse if that arrow should be burning as well. He roared above the cacophony of battle, and Molti did as he was bid and let loose his own arrow, aiming it towards where Swein directed him to.

He needed to keep an eye on the arrows. He needed to provide Molti with far more directions if he was going to get him to hit the archer.

He lowered his shield and pulled the guttering arrow from it, burning his hands in doing so. He cursed loudly and dropped the arrow into the sea, listening to its hiss as it hit the cold water. He'd intended to give the weapon to Molti but reconsidered as soon as he'd felt the heat.

He steadied himself and then lifted his foot to make the leap from the one ship to the other. For a heartbeat, he was airborne until he felt his foot impact with the wooden hull of the other vessel. Behind him, he heard a similar thud and knew that Molti had made the crossing as well.

Good. With Molti behind him, he felt secure. The ship was filled with a combination of Olof's warriors and his own, and he quickly realised that not one, but two of his sides craft had impacted the one ship. It wasn't as close to sinking as the ship he'd rammed or the one he'd just leapt from, but it was filled with fighting men and the flash of metal in the sunlight was menacing.

In the distance, he finally clapped eyes on Olaf, dismayed to find that he was beating back the attack by Olof and his ineffectual warriors. They'd struck the craft but had barely made an impact on Olaf's magnificent ship, the extremely long and high-sided Long Serpent. Swein knew that she was Olaf's pride and joy.

He cursed again, wishing that he'd not brought Olof along to the battle. If he'd been allowed to attack Olaf, he'd have inflicted far more damage and wouldn't be allowing Olaf to fight back. If he'd attacked Olaf first, Olaf would have died by now.

"How will we get across?" Molti shouted into his ear. Swein was momentarily stumped. He could see no way of ensuring that they made it safely to this ship and onto the next one.

"We'll have to fight our way through," he shouted back, raising his shield to deflect once more an arrow, this one not set alight but deadly all the same.

"Can't you find the archer?" he shouted to Molti, his temper getting the better of him.

"I can't see him, my Lord," was Molti's reasoned reply and Swein knew he was asking the impossible.

He held the shield high, feeling the ship rock with the weight of the men. He had a fear that any moment now, the ship was going to start to sink. He wanted to get off it long before that happened.

"We'll have to either run for it or swim our way along."

Molti shook his head vehemently.

"I'd much rather run my Lord. The sea isn't a forgiving mistress."

Looking into its dark depths, Swein could understand why Molti didn't want to risk swimming through the confusion of floating corpses, bloodied weapons and pieces of the ships that had been ripped apart.

"I agree. You fire arrows before us, and we'll have to make our way through this mess of men as best we can."

"Yes my Lord," Molti agreed, already holding an arrow at the bow. If only Swein could see where Olaf's archer was, he knew their endeavour would be far easier.

"Come on then," Swein shouted and he began to pick his way past the warring men as quickly as he could. Along the way, he held his shield before him even though it restricted his view. Without his byrnie, he needed to protect his body from the damn stray arrows that kept flying towards him. The tang of blood filled his nostrils alongside the smell of the sea, stinking men and the stench of death. Although he barreled through the fighting, he couldn't help but see the dead bodies, the permanently staring eyes of those who'd never fight again, and the fear-crazed eyes of those who knew they were about to die.

This battle was going to be hefty on casualties. To kill just one man, many men would lose their lives. He cursed Olaf once more. It was all his damn fault. He should have died four years ago, and then none of this would have been necessary. Both good warriors and bad would die today. There was no way of stopping the slaughter and Swein didn't want to stop now, even if he could have done.

Four long years. He would ensure that Olaf died no matter the cost to him concerning lost men and lost treasure.

From where his own ship had beached over the other vessel he heard a long drawn out cry of rage, almost as though the sea spoke, and then the shield wall of Olaf's, his five ships held closely together with ropes and sheer luck, lost one of their number. His own ship had fatally wounded the other, and he turned in awe, watching the men who went down with the ship, nearly all of them still engaged in a battle with an enemy. Did they not notice the ship sinking beneath them? Did they not feel the chill water as it swept up their legs?

He hoped Thorkell had fought his way free from Axe.

Immediately he felt the ship he was on lower in the water, and he saw that some of the men must have been aware of what was happening for they'd all made a late attempt to seek sanctuary on the ship to the side of them. Some men had managed to clatter aboard the ship he now stood on without being noticed, but he saw Thorkell trying to dispatch those who fought for Olaf as they fought with their wet clothing and their weapons to gain a purchase on the side of the high-sided vessel. Some, who made it to the edge of the ship, or even onto the ship, lost their balance and tumbled backwards into the water, their wet clothes making it impossible for them to return to the surface. They'd have a watery death.

Those who'd swum to Olaf's other ships were faring better, but the water still glowed with the combined reflection of the rising sun and the spilt blood of those with injuries.

His ship had returned to the water with an enormous surge of water splashing over the other ships, and now it held its place in the swirl of bustling activity. He braced himself for the reflected ricochet as his ship rebalanced but it still brought him to one knee. He felt the hiss of another arrow and silently thanked the intervention of his ship. He stood unsteadily, his shield above his head. He could make out men fighting inside his ship, but he moved on. He needed to get to Olaf.

"Can you not kill the damn archer?" he called to no one in particular, but still arrows thumped into his shield. It was growing heavy and ungainly with the projectiles sticking out from it and he'd still only made it half way across the ship. He could see Olaf fighting with a broad grin on his face within the Long Serpent but he was getting no closer to him, and he was starting to tire.

Rowing a ship all day and standing on it as it negotiated the waves was second nature to him. Trying to stay upright while the battle raged against him was far more exhausting.

The constant movement of the ships wasn't helping either. Every time a man stepped close to him he had to rebalance himself. He knew that tomorrow he'd ache all over. He wasn't looking forward to it, especially not when he considered that all his men would be in the same predicament and he intended to row home as well.

As if from nowhere a great gust of wind blew fiercely sending sparks from the fire raging in the ships to the left rushing towards him. A stray spark caught in his beard, the smell drifting to him in time that he could crush the tiny conflagration before it burnt his beard away and impacted his skin.

He sucked in a deep breath and then coughed as he choked on the ash. This battle was turning into a misery of perseverance.

"My Lord," a shrill cry caught his ears, and he wondered who was shouting for which Lord, the sound cut off with an agonised cry. Whoever it was would certainly not be needing their Lord now.

In the distance he caught a glimpse of those of Erik's ships that had tried to circle Olaf, they seemed to be floundering and were making no progress at all even though they only faced one of Olaf's ships. Behind him, he knew the rest of the ships were struggling just as much. He considered calling in his reserve force, but he didn't want to. Not yet. He thought his coalition were gaining against Olaf and provided he still thought that he didn't want to endanger any more of his men than he had to.

His shield before him, he finally reached the end of the ship he was navigating along. He viewed the imposing side of the Long Serpent and reconsidered his actions. How was he to gain access to the high-sided vessel? He didn't want to scurry over the side like a rat trying to make its way to dry ground.

He wiped sweat from his eyes while simultaneously shielding himself from the blow of an axe wielded by a wild-eyed man who had a huge gash across the top of his head. Swein could see the glistening insides of the man's head and lashed out with his own axe to swipe across the man's neck. The man stumbled and fell before him, his eyes never leaving his face.

Swein knew he'd done the man a favour by killing him because recovery from such a wound would be difficult, even if possible, and as his strange eyes had already shown, the low blow had probably affected his memory and his very being. Men with such grave injuries to their heads, if they survived, were often a blight on their families. Still, he took no pleasure in the man's death, no matter that he was one of Olaf's warriors. He'd not come to put down men with such grievous injuries.

"Swein," Thorkell called, dragging him from his thoughts, and Swein looked at him. Thorkell had managed to drag two war chests towards the edge of the ship, and he was standing on them, ensuring that with them beneath his feet, he'd be able to scramble onto Long Serpent.

Swein rushed to his side, his resolve redoubled.

He could still kill Olaf.

He stood on the war chests, Thorkell holding his legs steady, and clasping his axe, and he grabbed the high prow of the ship, around the serpent head that crowned it, it's black eyes looking intently at him as though daring him to try and gain admittance to her. He ignored the serpent and instead checked to see if it was possible to sneak onto the ship. Men were engaged in mortal combat along the war chests used as benches by the shipmen, but the space before him was remarkably clear of any of the enemy.

He could see that Olof stood, still trying to fight his way towards Olaf, but Olaf was surrounded by the finest of his warriors, and at his side, a man had an arrow pointed directly at Swein's head.

He ducked his head quickly, below the serpent head and cursed every God he could think of.

"What is it Swein?" Thorkell asked, agitation in his voice.

He quickly explained the problem and Thorkell called Molti to their side.

"You'll have to go up first, shoot a few arrows at the archer and distract him while Swein slides over the side."

Molti turned to gather an arrow from the few on his back but came up empty handed, his face showed panic as he realised he'd used all his arrows.

Swein cursed once more. Nothing about this was proving to be easy to accomplish. Above their heads, another arrow whistled before embedding itself into the ship's mast. Molti grinned and rushed through the swell of fighting men to pull the arrow lose.

"You'll have to be quick my Lord," he cautioned, and Swein nodded to show he understood. If he made it onto Olaf's ship, it would be nothing short of one of the Christian God's miracles, but he needed to. He needed to ensure that all the dead men today had died for a good reason.

They both crouched on top of Thorkell's hastily constructed raised platform and waited for the telltale hiss of an arrow heading their way. When nothing happened, Swein showed his head to speed up their attack and was immediately rewarded with an arrow aimed towards him. Molti stood the moment the arrow had passed and shot the retrieved weapon back towards Olaf while Swein gripped the serpent head once more and eased his body over the side of the ship with the aid of a boost from Thorkell. He slid into the base of the ship and regained his breath.

A thud beside him was his axe being thrown over by Thorkell. He wasn't sure if the archer had seen his illicit entry onto the ship but he wasn't about to wait and find out. Another thud and his shield joined him.

He righted his helm once his shield was before him and his axe back in his hand. He waited for an arrow to hit his shield and when it didn't, he began to make his way towards the widest part of the ship, where Olaf and his men were soundly beating off the attack from Olof.

Swein saw that Olof had been unable to attack the side of the vessel as well as he'd managed to attack his own intended target, and even now Olof's ship floundered beside Olaf's. The sides were so high that Olof's men had to make their own temporary structures to breach the Long Serpent. Swein once more berated himself for allowing Olof so much control over the battle.

To the left of Olaf's ship, those of Erik's ships that hadn't fallen victim to the flaming arrows were trying to help those on the two burning ships and seemed completely unaware that there was even a battle taking place. Swein swallowed his frustration. If he let it show now, he was more likely to make another foolish decision.

In front of him, he could see Erik and his ships fiercely attacking the two ships that Olaf had formed into a shield wall. Erik was on board the furthest ship, but the ship that separated them was firmly in the hand of Olaf's warriors who were pouring over from the vessel at their back to reinforce their friends and comrades.

The battle was too close to call. He needed to do something decisive to ensure his victory.

The ship boards behind him buckled, and he turned in surprise to see Molti and Thorkell at his back.

"The archer's distracted by what's happening over there," Thorkell said pointing and Swein glanced where he pointed. The archer was caught up in his attempts to kill Erik.

"Good," Swein grunted. "Now let's get closer to Olaf while we can."

The three of them, with more men pouring over the side of the ship, began to make their way towards Olaf and his greatest warriors.

The ship was over sixty feet in length, and it took long moments to get even within striking distance of any of the men who were all bunched around the central mast, where Olaf stood goading them all on and fighting amongst them. Olof and his men were trying to swarm amongst Olaf's men, but they had a shield wall firmly in place, their shields overlapping tightly with the other men side by side to them and all that Olof was doing was becoming exhausted against the impenetrable wall. Swein didn't know how to breach it and the closer he got the more men were getting in his way.

He wanted a free run at Olaf, but he wasn't going to get one.

He slashed with his axe at any man who came near him no longer mindful of whether they were Olaf or Olof's men, his men. They just needed to be gone.

The wet sounds of his axe impacting the chests of men, the necks of men emboldened Swein, and he felt possessed by an inner calm.

He could do this. He would kill Olaf. He just needed to get close enough to him first.

He was a man with vengeance on his mind, and he wouldn't be denied. Not again.

The ship shifted beneath his feet, sending him off balance as he slashed at the unprotected back of a man's neck but his weapon still bit deep, felling the man without the need to reposition himself.

The deck was slippery with blood and gore, but he pressed ever forwards, the reassuring grunts and groans from his companions following him wherever he went. It felt as though half the morning had passed, but when he took a deep shuddering breath as the space before him momentarily cleared, he realised that little time had gone by, the sun hung low on the horizon, nowhere close to midday.

It was a gory daybreak but one that was surely worth the planning and risks he'd taken. He worked his way nearer to Olof. He was the closest warrior to where Olaf was surrounded by his shield men. Swein could tell that he was a great warrior, it was simply that Olaf's men were even fiercer, more deadly and they had more at stake than Olof, and that ferocity could be sensed in every strike they made, every stabbing action, every hiss of an arrow.

Swein was so close to Olaf and his archer that it was impossible for the archer to sight at him. He finally lowered his shield from above his head, circling his aching shoulders as he did so. It wasn't natural to fight with his shield so high, and his neck was starting to pulse with pain.

Olaf fought with his men now, no longer content to wait in their midst for them to fight free from the attackers. Swein could hear his deep voice as he battled his men but he still couldn't see him. The attackers were too tightly bunched together and beneath their feet, too many bodies encumbered the slippery surface. The heat from a flaming archer hissed past his face, and he cursed. What fresh opponent was this?

The arrow stuck in the mast at the centre of the ship, flames greedily licking the old wood and making their way up towards the furled sail. The sail, held tightly against the wood, ready for the planned escape in the early morning dawn, immediately caught fire, the ropes fraying with a breath of flame, and the entire sail igniting within a heartbeat. It rained burning ash and fragments of seasoned, stinking cloth onto the warriors who fought beside Olaf, but not one of them flicked a stray flame from their clothing. They had only one objective, only one desire. To protect Olaf.

Into his ear, he heard Thorkell's voice,

"Erik my Lord."

He breathed and looked to where he knew Erik had last been fighting. He was smirking, with delight on his face, a bow and arrow in his hand. It was Erik that Swein had to thank for almost scorching his face and for setting alight Olaf's ship.

The heat from the flames intensified, men's faces dripping with sweat, but not once did their concentration lapse. In all the years of training men in the trelleborgs, Swein had never yet encountered such devotion, such single-minded determination.

Olaf knew how to lead and inspire loyalty. Swein thought he'd learned harsh lessons from his own father's failure to learn about the minds of men, but Olaf could teach him many more lessons. A pity really that he had to die.

More and more arrows hissed passed Swein, and he wondered whether Erik was trying to kill him, not Olaf. From his greater distance, Erik could more precisely determine the ebb and flow of the battle but the only way he could influence it was with arrows, flaming or not.

He hoped Erik didn't hit Olaf.

Along the length of the ships, a great cry of dismay reached Swein's ears, and he turned to see that another of the ships was slowly sinking. The ship had been impacted by one of his own vessels, and its work was finally complete.

As the ship listed, its occupants tried to either reach for safety or paid no heed to what was happening but continued fighting. Swein admired those men the most, but he didn't have long to do so before he felt cold metal on the side of his face. He spun his head slowly and met the gaze of a massive warrior, his half toothless sneer filling Swein's bowels with fear.

He knew this man. He was almost as lethal in battle as Olaf was.

With lightening quick reflexes, he worked his axe beneath the blade of the seax and forced the glittering weapon away from his eyes. He didn't need to be repaid with the same injury inflicted on the English jarl during their failed attack in the Shetlands.

The man, Harth, Swein suddenly remembered his name, glowered with rage, but in the next moment was sent spinning backwards as one of Erik's arrows embedded itself in his shoulder. Swein didn't take the time to consider how close the weapon had come to hitting him instead. Taking advantage of the warrior's downfall, he bent low and sliced his axe at the man's neck. Blood gushed immediately as Harth, too dazed to put up a defence, lay on the ship's deck.

And that was it. Swein was now within the shield wall, and all he needed to do was find Olaf and with Erik's long distance help it didn't appear as though it was going to take long. Arrows flew into the shield wall, and men died where they stood, or stumbled from the deck and splashed over the high sides into the water beyond, until only Olof, Swein, Thorkell, Molti and Dyri remained, all five of them facing a suddenly bereft Olaf.

Not that Olaf showed any fear, not at all.

He only lowered his blade, but not his shield that still protected his body from the seeking arrows of Erik, and met each man squarely in the eye. Swein expected his death to be written all over his face, but it wasn't, his cocky demeanour still more evident than any fear. Swein could only hope that he met his death so well.

"All this just for me?" Olaf called to the men, his voice only just reaching their ears, and intentionally so.

Swein calmed himself for a moment and then replied. He really didn't want Olaf to know how desperate he was for this moment.

"Your ally took the blade intended for you last time, and it's only fitting that you take it now."

Olaf swung his gaze to meet his own; his blond hair dripped with the blood of dead men and the ash from the fire that had burnt itself out above his head. His eyes were keen and interested.

"Lord Leofwine?" he queried, and Swein found himself nodding. Now was not the time for conversation and yet it was Olaf's last moments, and it seemed as though he was going to spend the time chatting.

"He's a great lord now, invaluable to the King of England. I know he'll avenge his wound."

"I doubt he'll have the opportunity to," Swein answered abruptly, and Olaf's eyes blazed with fury.

"It was never his fault that you were too short-sighted to wait for wealth and gold, and that I not only gained it but also gained the trust and goodwill of the English king."

"Goodwill earns you nothing," Swein retorted angrily. Good-will had done him no service in his dealings with Olaf.

"You shall see my Lord," Olaf answered ominously, and then he raised his axe and turned towards him.

"Who would like to try first?" he asked, stepping towards the assembled men and then dancing out of their reach again.

Olof looked at Swein, his desperation written all over his face. Swein licked his lips. He wanted this far more than Olof but could he afford to take the risk? Olaf wasn't even wounded; all the blood that mingled with his hair had come from other men. Should he let Olof at least try and kill the Norwegian King, at the least exhaust him so that the fight was easier for Swein?

No, he thought. To gain the renown of killing Olaf, he would have to make the killing blow himself.

"I'll not try first," he said, stepping three steps forward to meet Olaf on the raised platform in the middle of his ship. "I'll start and finish the battle," his voice strong enough to reach everyone who fought on in the other engagements taking place up and down the ships. He wanted everyone to know that he, Swein, King of Denmark, had killed Olaf.

Olaf merely grinned, delight on his face.

"You can bloody well try," he offered, moving to meet Swein's attacking posture while Swein ignored the howling cry of anger that erupted from Olof's lips.

Both men were similarly equipped, with axes, shields and helms, nothing else. It would be a battle of skill and prowess. Neither had any advantage over the other.

Quickly, Swein realised he needed to draw first blood, to make Olaf doubt himself, and he lashed out with his axe to aim a blow at the arm that held the shield. He almost connected but Olaf spun out of his way at the last possible moment, and Swein slightly overbalanced as he turned back to face his adversary.

He slashed wildly with his axe, hoping to connect with Olaf and also keep him at bay while he regained his composure. Men had stopped their own attacks on the other ships, and many were standing, watching, enemy and ally alike. Swein felt his heart beat quicker.

He needed to get this done and quickly.

He parried a blow from Olaf's axe with his shield and then simultaneously he tried to slice an opening into Olaf's exposed stomach, but he only managed to nick the very side of his body, as he struggled to deflect the weight of Olaf's axe, and no blood poured forth from the wound.

He was breathing very heavily now, his axe a huge weight in his arms. He almost wished he'd brought his seax or his sword with him, anything that gave him more maneuverability and was lighter to swing.

Olaf taunted him with a chuckle. He must have interpreted Swein's languid movements as a sign that he was slowing and weakening.

Suddenly his rage, held in check for so much of the morning, poured through him as though a beast had awakened inside him, and he rushed at Olaf, his movements careful and considered but driven by anger that had been nestled deep inside his stomach, like a wyrm and its egg. He slashed his axe from left to right, right to left, up and down and even high, as though he was going to slice his opponents nose from his face.

Olaf tried to keep up with the movements, but even he was weakening through exhaustion. Axe, shield, shield and axe all four weapons moved as though in a blur, and Swein wondered if it looked as though the weapons and the men had all joined into one fearful monster, trying to attack itself, because that was how it felt to be deep within the struggle.

He felt Olaf's heated breath on his face, his shield slamming into his own head and it didn't hurt, not at all, and neither did it blur his vision.

He slammed his own shield into Olaf's nose and was rewarded at last with a fine spray of blood from his broken nose. He didn't even allow himself to smile, but continued to hammer his shield and his axe against Olaf. He'd given up all pretense of using his shield defensively. It was a weapon, and he would use it against Olaf to smash and bruise his body.

A delighted ripple of laughter permeated the air as Olaf fought back just as hard, and then he stepped back, his breath harsh in his throat, his hand raised for a moment's respite that Swein felt honour bound to allow. He too needed to take the time to breathe before he considered his next move. Only suddenly Olaf was staggering backwards, veering dangerously closely to the side of his vessel, his balance all gone, and his hand clutched around something sticking out of his chest.

Swein howled with rage and turned to glare at Erik. Still, on his ship, he'd taken their brief moment of truce as an invitation to fire directly on Olaf, and he'd struck home. Olaf was watching Swein with a triumphant smirk on his face. He knew what denying him his death would do to him.

All those years, wasted as he tried to find the means to kill him once and for all.

He spun once more, his eyes finally lacing with pain, and Swein, unable to stop himself stepped towards him, uncaring of the bloody bodies and slick floor, and sliced his axe clean across Olaf's stomach. Blood sprang instantly to the surface, although even Swein knew it hadn't been a killing blow.

"Lord Swein," Olaf bubbled as blood flecked his mouth and beard.

"You always were an honourable bastard, to kill a man who's already dead takes great skill."

Swein howled with rage and anger. His axe raised to hit him again and again but with a grin on his lips, Olaf staggered to the side of his ship and hauled himself over the edge of the vessel.

Swein rushed to the side of the ship and watched Olaf disappear quickly from view as he took his shield and axe with him, his head tilted backwards so that he could watch Swein until the water clouded his view.

Swein watched him go angrily.

This should have been his kill.

Not Erik's.

EPILOGUE
After the Battle of Svoldor
AD999

Swein washed his face once more in the chill waters that swirled around his ship. The water was bloody cold, but it served the dual purpose of both keeping him alert and of wiping the sweat and blood from his face and his beard. He took especial care to ensure that his blond beard was clear of all flecks of blood. It was one thing to wear his beard so sharply that it almost mirrored his pointed chin and masked his birth mark, it was quite another for it to be dripping with the blood of his enemies.

His body trembled with the after effects of the battle, and he felt a little clumsy and foolish both. He was used to combat. This should no longer happen to him. But, and this was what he needed to remind himself, despite the vast number of men he'd taken to meet with Olaf, it was only because Olaf had died that they'd won. Before that event, it had been too close to call. It had been possible that Olaf could fight his way clear and live to see another day.

It had taken a tremendous effort on his part to ensure that Olaf had died. It had given him great satisfaction to watch his body slump after the slice of his blade and then slowly tumble into the still grey waters beneath them. That he hadn't even broken his fast yet, that morning only added to his enjoyment.

It had been easy in the end.

But it had been a very close battle.

Olaf's men were so well skilled and so well trained that any who came against them, even the men from the trelleborg's, were hard pressed to beat them. He'd watched Axe sail away with the remaining men of his ship still alive, and he'd known there and then that he'd left a scheming, vengeful man alive but he'd had no energy at all to go after the only retreating ship.

Neither could he summon the strength to call his men to row after the survivors. Fighting on the water was fraught with so many difficulties; just standing upright exhausted legs and backs when the water was even a little rough. Swein had spent much of his time on board ships, and yet he thought this was the greatest test of his skill yet.

Dyri slumped down beside him, sitting with his back against the side of their ship on top of one of the many war chests they'd hauled on board their own craft.

"My Lord," he said, his voice dripping with his exhaustion. "As you requested, we have one survivor for you. His name is Finn."

Swein nodded to show he understood but even that movement exhausted him. He needed to sleep, desperately.

"He knew the English jarl?" he finally managed to spit, and Dyri smirked as Thorkell led the man towards them, not caring that he held him by his hair and that he was more being dragged than escorted. His legs were crashing into any unsuspecting fool who was unaware of what was happening.

"He met him, he should know how to reach him."

Swein felt a tired smile on his face. Killing Olaf had only been part of his endeavours. The other half? Well, he still had an English lordling to kill. If he'd not been on Shetland four years ago, Olaf would have been dead and Swein wouldn't have been forced to spend the last four years listening to stories of Olaf's valour and his Christianizing ways in the northern lands. It had made him crave the ways of the Old Gods more and more, so much so that men still thought him a pagan, for all that he wasn't. He simply didn't see the need to pry into the belief of his people. Provided they tithed and supported him, as they should, he was happy with whomever they chose to worship.

He knew many of the priests who worked amongst the men and women of his land decried his attitude, but he could easily silence them if he needed to.

He blamed the English man for the uncertainties of the last four years and craved his death almost as much as he had Olaf's. But there was more, as well. His ambitions knew no bounds now that he had his two firm allies, and Olaf was dead. It would once more be safe to leave his lands and use the troops from his trelleborgs to grow his empire. He harboured a thought that England would make an excellent addition to the area he could now claim in Norway as well as his hold on Denmark.

He was no longer a young man, but he fancied he had many more years ahead of him. His sons were growing well, finally at an age where he found them interesting, and he had great plans, albeit secret ones, on how he could ensure both boys gained an empire once he did finally die.

The man before him had fear-filled eyes, and Swein noticed the splotches on his fingers. That more than explained why the man had been so easy to capture during the battle. He was no warrior, but a scribe. Swein grinned with delight, causing the man to shrink further away from him until he came up against the legs of Thorkell and could no longer go any further backwards.

"What's your name?" he asked roughly, enjoying the growing fear on the man's face. He was slight and had the appearance of one of the monks of the new God. Swein almost wished he was less exhausted and more likely to take the time to goad the man, but he wanted to deliver his message and have him gone from here as soon as possible.

"Finn my Lord," the man replied, his voice cracking even as he spoke. Swein was surprised that someone so weak as Finn had survived in Olaf's collection of warriors. All the men must have well liked him.

"You knew Olaf well?" he pressed. Finn paused for a long moment, as though he was sizing up the request.

"I did my Lord, yes. I've been his scribe since before his attack on England. I've written great long tales of his exploits, but I fear they may be lost at the bottom of the sea." There was real regret in his voice and Swein almost laughed with delight. It was strange to think of him mourning his bits of parchment and his stories of Olaf as opposed to Olaf himself.

"You met the English Jarl?" he interjected, fearful that he would be subjected to a long lamentation about the lost writing.

Once more Finn considered his answer.

"Do you mean the Lord Leofwine? The man you wounded on Shetland?"

"Of course I do, you damn fool. Did you know him?"

"I met him, my Lord, yes."

"And you'd be able to seek him out for me?"

The man's body visibly sagged with relief at those words and he almost fell over his own tongue in his eagerness to reply.

"Of course I could my Lord Swein."

"Good, I'll let you go once we return to Denmark. You can take ship and go to England. I want you to deliver a message to the English Jarl and his King for me."

"It would be my pleasure, my Lord," the man managed to whimper, but Swein was no longer listening to him. In his head, he was composing the next words he wanted to utter.

"You're to tell him this, and ensure he knows it comes from me."

Once more the slight man bobbed his head, and Swein had the stray thought that one day his head might well bob off his shoulders.

"I will be coming for England soon."

Finn's eyes weren't the only ones that bored into his own as he uttered those words, but Swein could only grin at finally voicing his desires after so long.

"I'll be coming for England soon, remember that," Swein repeated and then he closed his eyes and let the gentle swell of the sea rock him to sleep.

He'd be doing nothing until he'd rested his body and slept for a week.

HISTORICAL NOTES

And so to Denmark!

I've been fascinated for many years by the Viking Age in the Scandinavian countries. My favourite country is Iceland – the idea of those intrepid men and women peopling a land that was bereft of almost everything – inspires me, as does the development of their society. There aren't many countries where their early years are quite so well documented. And that love of Iceland has translated itself into my fantasy series, The Dragon of Unison, but now I'm turning my hand to something a little more historical with Swein.

So what can be said about Swein? Unlike England at this time period, the main source for events in Denmark is either the highly prejudiced work of Adam of Bremen, or the much later literary works that came from Iceland by Snori Sturllison (great name). Between the two, it's almost possible to piece together the events that happened in Denmark in this time, but in many ways it's almost a step back to the earlier Anglo-Saxon kingdoms in terms of what is known and what is simply wild conjecture. The sagas provide a wealth of information and whilst many debate whether they are a literary record, or an historical one, they are an invaluable, if somewhat dry account, of life at that time and their attention to detail will both annoy and inspire.

They are not easy to piece together and neither is the dating secure but for once I've allowed myself to take off my 'strictly historical fact head' and accept some of the ideas from the sagas.

Without them it would be difficult to offer a version of Swein's life.

There's a great article you can almost read in full on Google books by Peter Sawyer about the literary history of Swein and how it's more than likely affected today's understanding of the man. As with all historical figures, the bias that infects the writer is as important to understand as the information they actually provide.

What can be said is that Swein rose in rebellion against his father, Harald Bluetooth and took his throne, and was instrumental in his death. We don't know why. Harald converted to Christianity and built a church in which he placed the bodies of his father and mother, disinterring them from their mound burials. He seems to have understood the need to build and maintain defensive earthworks – the Danevirke and also the trelleborg fortresses, which are fascinating and still being discovered and deciphered. A few theories surround them, I quite like the idea that Swein built them to allow his invasion of England to take place, but dating shows that some at least were built in the 980's and so it might be a bit presumptuous unless of course Swein had his eye on conquering somewhere from the time he claimed his father's throne.

As to Swein himself, his later years seem to be far better documented than his early years as King. It is accepted that he raided England in 994 with Olaf but why Olaf made an alliance with Æthelred II while Swein didn't, does lend itself to some sort of disagreement between the men. Certainly Swein was keen to kill Olaf at Svolder because he wanted to claim Olaf's land for himself. Both men were Christian and so it wasn't a war of religion but rather about land.

Rumours abound about what happened after the Battle of Svolder, and just like King Arthur, Olaf of Norway was expected to return from wherever he'd been hiding since faking his own death. As such, and despite my best intentions, I've had to leave his death with a question mark hanging over it. Anything else seems a little wrong.

And finally, as much as this book is about Swein of Denmark, it is my Swein of Denmark as envisaged in the Earls of Mercia series and so, I'm afraid, I've added my own interpretation to his literary heritage and I humbly apologize for that!

CAST OF CHARACTERS

Harald Bluetooth, King of Denmark and Swein's father c.958-c.986

Married **Gyrid Olafsdottir**

Thrya – Harald's daughter/Swein's sister – married Styrbjörn the Strong
Swein Forkbeard c.960-1014
Haakon (Swein's brother) c.961
Gytha (Swein's younger sister – married Pallig)

Swein Forkbeard
Married 1) Gunhild
Harald – his eldest son
Cnut – his second son

Married 2) Sigrid the Haughty, mother of Olof Skötkonung, King of Sweden

Molti – Swein's warrior
Dryi – Swein's warrior
Thorkell the Tall – Jomsviking
Haaken – King of Norway (Harald's ally and then enemy)
Olaf Tryggvason – to be King of Norway
Axe and Horic are his men

Jarl Sigrid – Jarl of Shetland and Orkney

Ealdorman Leofwine – Ealdorman of the Hwicce (English kingdom)

King Æthelred II – King of England

MEET THE AUTHOR

I'm an author of fantasy (viking age/dragon themed) and historical fiction (Early English, Vikings and the British Isles as a whole before the Norman Conquest), born in the old Mercian kingdom at some point since the end of Anglo-Saxon England.

I write A LOT. You've been warned! Find me at https://mjporterauthor.com and @coloursofunison on twitter.

Books by M J Porter (in series reading order)

Gods and Kings Series
Pagan Warrior
Pagan King
Warrior King

The Tenth Century
The Lady of Mercia's Daughter
A Conspiracy of Kings (Coming soon)
Kingmaker
The King's Daughters

Chronicles of the English
Brunanburh
Of Kings and Half-Kings
The Second English King

The Mercian Brexit
The First Queen of England (audiobook available)
The First Queen of England Part 2 (audiobook available)
The First Queen of England Part 3

The King's Mother

The Queen Dowager
Once A Queen

<u>The Earls of Mercia</u>
The Earl of Mercia's Father
The Danish King's Enemy
Swein: The Danish King (side king)
Northman Part 1
Wulfstan: An Anglo-Saxon Thegn (side story)
Northman Part 2
The King's Earl
Cnut: The Conqueror (full length side story)
The Earl of Mercia
The English Earl
The Earl's King
Viking King

<u>The Dragon of Unison Series</u>
Hidden Dragon
Dragon Gone
Dragon Alone
Dragon Ally
Dragon Lost
Dragon Bond

As JE Porter
The Innkeeper

Made in the USA
Monee, IL
15 July 2023

39312934R00085